A Little Princess

A Little Princess

Frances Hodgson Burnett

Edited by Kathryn Lindskoog
Illustrated by Barbara Chitouras

P&R PUBLISHING
P.O. BOX 817 • PHILLIPSBURG • NEW JERSEY 08865-0817

**A study guide to this edition
of A Little Princess is available
from P&R Publishing
(1 800-631-0094)**

Library of Congress Cataloging-in-Publication Data

Burnett, Frances Hodgson, 1849–1924.
    A little princess / Frances Hodgson Burnett ; edited by Kathryn Lind-skoog ; illustrated by Barbara Chitouras.
        p. cm — (Classics for young readers)
    Reprint. Originally published: Sisters, Ore. : Multnomah, c1993.
    Summary: Sara Crewe, a pupil at Miss Minchin's London school, is left in poverty when her father dies but is later rescued by a myterious bene-factor.
    ISBN 0-87552-727-2 (pbk.)
    [1. Boarding schools—Fiction. 2. Schools—Fiction. 3. Orphans—Fiction. 4. London (England)—Fiction. 5. England—Fiction.] I. Lindskoog, Kathryn Ann. II. Chitouras, Barbara, ill. III. Title. IV. Series.

PZ7.B934 Lg 2002b
[Fic]—dc21

                                             2001051029

CONTENTS

·

1
SARA

ONCE ON A dark winter's day, when the yellow fog hung so thick and heavy in the streets of London that the lamps were lighted and the shop windows blazed as they do at night, an odd-looking little girl sat in a cab with her father and was driven slowly through the big thoroughfares.

She sat with her feet tucked under her and leaned against her father, staring out the window at people with a queer old-fashioned thoughtfulness in her big eyes.

She was such a little girl that one did not expect to see such a look on her small face. It would have been an old look for a child of twelve, and Sara Crewe was only seven. The fact was, however, that she was always dreaming and thinking odd things and could not herself remember any time when she had not been thinking things about grown-up people and the world they belonged to. She felt as if she had lived a long, long time.

At this moment she was remembering the voyage she had just made from Bombay with her father, Captain Crewe. She was thinking of the big ship, of the children playing about on the hot deck, and of some young officers' wives who used to laugh at the things she said.

Principally, she was thinking of what a queer thing it was that at one time one was in India in the blazing sun, and then in the middle of the ocean, and then driving in a strange vehicle through strange streets where the day was as dark as the night. She found this so puzzling that she moved closer to her father.

"Papa," she said in a low, mysterious little voice which was almost a whisper. "Papa."

"What is it, darling?" Captain Crewe answered, holding her closer and looking down into her face.

"Is this the place?" Sara whispered, cuddling still closer. "Is it, Papa?"

"Yes, little Sara, it is. We have reached it at last." And though she was only seven years old, she knew that he felt sad when he said it.

It seemed to her many years since he had begun to prepare her mind for "the place," as she always called it. Her mother had died when Sara was born, so she had never known or missed her. Her rich, handsome father seemed to be the only relation she had in the world. They had always played together and been fond of each other. She had always lived in a beautiful bungalow and had been used to many servants who bowed when they spoke to her and called her "Missee Sahib" and gave her her own way in everything. She had toys and pets and a helper called an "ayah" who worshiped her, and she had gradually learned that people who were rich had these things. That, however, was all she knew about it.

During her short life only one thing had troubled her, and that thing was "the place" she was to be taken to some day. The climate of India was bad for English children, and as soon as possible they were sent away—generally to England and to school. She had seen other children go away and had heard their fathers and mothers talk about the letters they received from them.

"Couldn't you go to that place with me, Papa?" she had asked when she was five years old. "Couldn't you go to school, too? I would help you with your lessons."

"But you will not have to stay for a very long time, little Sara," he had always said. "You will go to a nice house where there will be a lot of little girls, and you will play together, and I will send you plenty of books, and you will grow so fast that it will seem scarcely a year before you are big enough and clever enough to come back and take care of Papa." She had liked to think of that.

"Well, Papa," she said softly, "if we are here I suppose we must be resigned."

He laughed at her old-fashioned speech and kissed her. He was really not at all resigned himself. He felt he should be a lonely fellow when, on his return to India, he went into his bungalow knowing he would not see the small figure in its white frock come forward to meet him. So he held her closely in his arms as the cab rolled into the big, dull square in which stood the house that was their destination.

It was a big brick house, exactly like all the others there, but on the front door there shone a brass plate on which was engraved in black letters:

Miss Minchin
Select Seminary for Young Ladies

"Here we are, Sara," said Captain Crewe, making his voice sound as cheerful as possible. Then he lifted her out of the cab and they mounted the steps and rang the bell. Sara often thought afterward that the house was somehow exactly like Miss Minchin. It was respectable, but everything in it was ugly; the very armchairs seemed to have hard bones in them. In the hall everything was hard and polished—even the moon face on the tall clock in the corner had a severe varnished look. The drawing room they were ushered into was covered by a carpet with a square pattern upon it, the chairs were square, and a heavy marble timepiece stood upon the heavy marble mantel.

As she sat in one of the stiff mahogany chairs, Sara cast one of her quick looks about her.

"I don't like it, Papa," she said. "But then I dare say soldiers— even brave ones—don't really like going into battle." Captain Crewe laughed outright. He was young and full of fun, and he never tired of hearing Sara's queer speeches.

"Oh, little Sara, what shall I do when I have no one to say solemn things to me! No one else is as solemn as you are."

"But why do solemn things make you laugh so?" inquired Sara.

"Because you are such fun when you say them." And then suddenly he swept her into his arms and kissed her hard, stopping laughing all at once and looking almost as if tears had come into his eyes.

It was just then that Miss Minchin entered the room. She was very like her house, Sara felt: tall and dull and respectable and ugly. She had large, cold eyes, and a large, cold smile. It spread itself into a very large smile when she saw Sara and Captain Crewe. She had heard from the lady who had recommended her school to him that he was willing to spend a great deal of money on his little daughter.

"It will be a great privilege to have charge of such a beautiful and promising child, Captain Crewe," she said, taking Sara's hand and stroking it. "Lady Meredith has told me of her unusual cleverness. A clever child is a great treasure in an establishment such as mine."

Sara stood quietly with her eyes fixed upon Miss Minchin's

face. She was thinking something odd, as usual.

Why does she say I am a beautiful child? she was thinking. *I am not beautiful at all. Colonel Grange's little girl, Isobel, is beautiful. She has dimples and rose-colored cheeks and long hair the color of gold. I have short black hair and green eyes; besides which, I am a thin child and not fair in the least. I am one of the ugliest children I ever saw. She is beginning by telling a story.*

Sara was mistaken, however, in thinking she was an ugly child. She was slim, rather tall for her age, and had an intense, attractive little face. Her hair was heavy and black and only curled at the tips; her eyes were greenish gray, it is true, but they were big, wonderful eyes with long, black lashes, and though she did not like the color of them, many other people did. Still, she was not at all elated by Miss Minchin's flattery.

I would be telling a story if I said she was beautiful, Sara thought, *and I would know I was telling a story. What did she say that for?*

After she had known Miss Minchin longer she learned why she had said it. She discovered that she said the same thing to each papa and mamma who brought a child to her boarding school.

Sara stood near her father and listened while he and Miss Minchin talked. Sara was to be what was known as "a parlor boarder," and she was to enjoy even greater privileges than parlor boarders usually did. She was to have a pretty bedroom and sitting room of her own. She was to have a pony and a carriage, and a maid to take the place of the *ayah* who cared for her in India.

"I am not in the least anxious about her education," Captain Crewe laughed. "The difficulty will be to keep her from learning too fast and too much. She is always sitting with her little nose burrowing into books. She doesn't read them, Miss Minchin; she gobbles them up as if she were a little wolf

11

instead of a little girl. She is always starving for new books to gobble, and she wants grown-up books—great big fat ones—French and German as well as English—history and biography and poets, and all sorts of things. Drag her away from her books when she reads too much. Make her ride her pony or go out and buy a new doll. She ought to play more with dolls."

"Papa," said Sara, "you see, if I went out and bought a new doll every few days I should have more than I could be fond of. Dolls ought to be intimate friends. Emily is going to be my intimate friend."

Captain Crewe looked at Miss Minchin and Miss Minchin looked at Captain Crewe.

"Who is Emily?" she inquired.

"Tell her, Sara," Captain Crewe said, smiling.

Sara's green-gray eyes looked solemn and soft as she answered, "She is a doll I haven't got yet. She is a doll Papa is going to buy for me. We are going out together to find her. I have called her Emily. She is going to be my friend when Papa is gone. I want her to talk to about him."

Miss Minchin's large, fishy smile became very flattering. "What an original child!" she said. "What a darling little creature!"

"Yes," said Captain Crewe, drawing Sara close. "She is a darling. Take great care of her for me, Miss Minchin."

Sara stayed with her father at his hotel until he sailed away again to India. They went out and visited many big shops together, and bought a great many more things than Sara needed. But Captain Crewe was a young man who wanted his little girl to have everything she admired and everything he admired himself, so between them they collected a wardrobe much too grand for a child of seven. There were velvet dresses trimmed with costly furs, and lace dresses, and embroidered ones, and hats with great, soft ostrich feathers, and ermine coats and muffs, and boxes of tiny gloves and handkerchiefs and silk stockings in such abundant supplies that the polite young women behind the counters whispered to each other that the odd little girl with the big, solemn eyes must be a foreign princess.

And at last they found Emily, but they went to a number of toy shops and looked at a great many dolls before they discovered her.

"I want her to look as if she isn't a doll really," Sara said. "I want her to look as if she listens when I talk to her. The trouble with dolls, Papa"—and she put her head to one side and reflected as she said it—"the trouble with dolls is that they never seem to *hear*." So they looked at big ones and little ones—at dolls with black eyes and dolls with blue, at dolls with brown curls and dolls with golden braids, dolls dressed and dolls undressed.

"You see," Sara said when they were examining one who had no clothes. "If, when I find her, she has no frocks, we can take her to a dressmaker and have her things made to fit."

After a number of disappointments they decided to walk and look in at the shop windows. Sara suddenly clutched her father's arm.

"Oh, Papa!" she cried. "There is Emily!"

A flush had risen to her face and there was an expression in her green-gray eyes as if she had just recognized someone.

"She is actually waiting there for us!" she said. "Let us go in to her."

"Dear me," said Captain Crewe, "I feel as if we ought to have someone to introduce us."

"You must introduce me and I will introduce you," said Sara. "But I knew her the minute I saw her—so perhaps she knew me, too."

Emily had a very intelligent expression in her eyes when Sara took her in her arms. She was a large doll, but not too large to carry about easily. She had naturally curling golden-brown hair, and her eyes were a deep, clear, gray-blue, with soft, thick eyelashes.

"Of course," said Sara, looking into her face as she held her on her knee. "Of course, Papa, this is Emily."

So Emily was bought and actually taken to a children's shop and measured for a wardrobe as grand as Sara's own. She had lace frocks, too, and velvet and muslin ones, and hats and coats and beautiful lace-trimmed underwear, and gloves and handkerchiefs and furs.

"I should like her always to look as if she were a child with a good mother," said Sara. "I'm her mother, though I am going to make a companion of her."

Captain Crewe would have enjoyed the shopping tremendously, but a sad thought kept tugging at his heart. He got out of his bed in the middle of that night and went and stood looking down at Sara, who lay asleep with Emily in her arms. Her black hair was spread out on the pillow, and Emily's golden-brown hair mingled with it. Both of them had lace-ruffled nightgowns, and both had long eyelashes which lay on their cheeks.

"Ah, little Sara!" he said to himself. "I don't believe you know how much your daddy will miss you."

The next day he took her to Miss Minchin's and left her there. He was to sail away the next morning. He explained to Miss Minchin that his attorneys, Messrs. Barrow and Skipworth, had charge of his affairs in England and would pay the bills she sent in for Sara's expenses. He would write to Sara twice a week, and she was to be given every pleasure she asked for.

"She is a sensible little thing, and she never wants anything it isn't safe to give her," he said.

Then he went with Sara into her little sitting room to say goodbye. Sara sat on his knee and held the lapels of his coat in her small hands, and looked long and hard at his face.

"Are you learning me by heart, little Sara?" he said, stroking her hair.

"No," she answered. "I know you by heart. You are inside my heart." And they put their arms round each other and kissed as if they would never let each other go.

When the cab drove away from the door, Sara was watching from her sitting room, with her hands under her chin and her eyes following it until it had turned the corner of the square. Emily was sitting by her, and she looked after it, too. When Miss Minchin sent her sister, Miss Amelia, to see what the child was doing, she found she could not open the door.

"I have locked it," said a queer, polite little voice from inside. "I want to be quite by myself, if you please."

Miss Amelia was fat and dumpy, and stood in awe of her sister. She was really the better-natured person of the two, but she never disobeyed Miss Minchin. She went downstairs again, looking almost alarmed.

"I never saw such a funny, old-fashioned child, Sister," she said. "She has locked herself in, and she is not making the least bit of noise."

"It is much better than if she kicked and screamed, as some of them do," Miss Minchin answered. "I expected that a child as much spoiled as she is would set the whole house in an uproar."

"I've been opening her trunks and putting her things away," said Miss Amelia. "I never saw anything like them—sable and ermine on her coats, and fine lace on her underwear. You have seen some of her clothes. What do you think of them?"

"I think they are perfectly ridiculous," replied Miss Minchin, sharply. "But they will look very well at the head of the line when we take the girls to church on Sunday. She has been provided for as if she were a little princess."

Upstairs in the locked room Sara and Emily stared out the window at the corner round which the cab had disappeared, while somewhere Captain Crewe looked backward, waving and kissing his hand as if he could not bear to stop.

2
A FRENCH LESSON

WHEN SARA ENTERED the schoolroom the next morning everyone looked at her with wide, interested eyes. By that time every
pupil—from Lavinia Herbert, who was nearly thirteen and felt
quite grown up, to Lottie Legh, who was only four and the
baby of the school—had heard a great deal about her. They
knew she was Miss Minchin's star pupil and was considered a
credit to the establishment. One or two of them had even
caught a glimpse of her French maid, Mariette, who had
arrived the evening before. Lavinia had managed to pass Sara's
room when the door was open, and had seen Mariette opening a box.

"It was full of petticoats with lace frills on them—frills and
frills," she whispered to her friend Jessie as she bent over her
geography. "I saw her shaking them out. I heard Miss Minchin
say to Miss Amelia that her clothes were ridiculous for a child.
She has one of those petticoats on now. I saw it when she sat
down."

"She has silk stockings on!" whispered Jessie, bending over
her geography also. "And what little feet! I never saw such little
feet."

"Oh," sniffed Lavinia, spitefully, "that is the way her shoes are made. I don't think she is pretty at all. Her eyes are such a queer color."

"She isn't pretty as other pretty people are," said Jessie, stealing a glance across the room, "but she makes you want to look at her again. She has tremendously long eyelashes, but her eyes are almost green."

Sara was sitting quietly in her seat, waiting to be told what to do. She had been placed near Miss Minchin's desk. She was not embarrassed at all by the many pairs of eyes watching her. She was interested and looked back quietly at the children who looked at her. She wondered what they were thinking, and if they liked Miss Minchin, and if they cared for their lessons, and if any of them had a papa at all like her own. She had had a long talk with Emily about her papa that morning.

"He is on the sea now, Emily," she had said. "We must be great friends to each other and tell each other things. Emily, look at me. You have the nicest eyes I ever saw, but I wish you could speak."

She was a child full of imaginings and whimsical thoughts, and one of her fancies was that there would be a great deal of comfort in pretending that Emily was alive and really heard and understood. After Mariette had dressed her in her dark-blue schoolroom frock and tied her hair with a dark blue ribbon, she went to Emily, who sat in a chair of her own, and gave her a book.

"You can read that while I am downstairs," she said. And seeing Mariette looking at her curiously, she spoke to her with a serious little face.

"What I believe about dolls," she said, "is that they can do things they will not let us know about. If you stay in the room, Emily will just sit there and stare; but if you go out, she will begin to read, perhaps, or go and look out the window. Then if she heard either of us coming, she would just run back and jump into her chair and pretend she had been there all the time."

Mariette thought to herself how silly that was, but she had already begun to like this odd little girl who had such an intelligent small face and such perfect manners. She had taken care of children before who were not so polite. She was very much pleased with her new little mistress.

After Sara had sat in her seat in the schoolroom for a few minutes, being looked at by the pupils, Miss Minchin rapped in a dignified manner upon her desk.

"Young ladies," she said, "I wish to introduce you to your new companion." All the little girls rose in their places, and Sara rose also. "I shall expect you all to be very agreeable to Miss Crewe. She has just come to us from a great distance—in fact, from India."

The pupils bowed ceremoniously, Sara made a little curtsy, and then they sat down and looked at each other again.

"Sara," said Miss Minchin in her schoolroom manner, "come here to me." She had taken a book from the desk.

"As your papa has engaged a French maid for you," she began, "I conclude that he wishes you to make a special study of the French language."

"I think he engaged her," Sara said, "because he—he thought I would like her, Miss Minchin."

"I am afraid," said Miss Minchin, with a slightly sour smile, "that you have been a very spoiled little girl and always imagine that things are done because you like them. My impression is that your papa wished you to learn French."

If Sara had been older or less polite, she could have explained herself in a few words. But, as it was, she felt a flush rising on her cheeks. Miss Minchin was a severe and imposing

*"Young ladies, I wish to introduce you
to your new companion."*

person, and she seemed so absolutely sure that Sara knew nothing whatever of French that it would be almost rude to correct her. The truth was that Sara could not remember a time when she had not known French. Her mother had been a French woman, and Captain Crewe had loved her language, so it happened that Sara had always been familiar with it.

"I—I have never really learned French, but—but—" she began, trying shyly to make herself clear.

One of Miss Minchin's chief secret annoyances was that she did not speak French herself and wanted to conceal that irritating fact.

"That is enough," she said with polite tartness. "If you have not learned, you must begin at once. The French master, Monsieur Dufarge, will be here in a few minutes. Take this book and look at it until he arrives."

Sara's cheeks felt warm. She went back to her seat and opened the book. She looked at the first page with a grave face. She knew it would be rude to smile, but it was odd to find herself expected to study a page which told her that *le pere* meant "the father," and *la mere* meant "the mother."

"You look rather cross, Sara," Miss Minchin said. "I am sorry you do not like the idea of learning French."

"I am very fond of it," answered Sara, thinking she would try again. "But—"

"You must not say 'but' when you are told to do things," said Miss Minchin. "Look at your book again."

And Sara did so, and did not smile, even when she found that *le fils* meant "the son," and *le frere* meant "the brother." *When Monsieur Dufarge comes,* she thought, *I can make him understand.*

Monsieur Dufarge arrived shortly afterward, and he looked interested when his eyes fell upon Sara trying politely to seem absorbed in her little book of phrases.

"Is this a new pupil for me, madame?"

"Her papa—Captain Crewe—is very anxious that she should begin the language. But she does not seem to wish to learn," said Miss Minchin.

"I am sorry of that, mademoiselle," he said kindly to Sara. "Perhaps when we begin to study together, I may show you that it is a charming tongue."

Little Sara rose in her seat. She was beginning to feel desperate, as if she were almost in disgrace. She looked up into Monsieur Dufarge's intelligent face with her big, green-gray eyes. She began to explain quite simply in pretty and fluent French. Madame had not understood. She had not learned French exactly—not out of books—but people had always spoken it to her, and she had read it and written it along with English. Her papa loved it, and she loved it because he did. Her dear mamma, who had died when she was born, had been French. She would be glad to learn anything monsieur would teach her, but what she had tried to explain to madame was that she already knew the words in this book—and she held it out.

When she began to speak Miss Minchin winced and sat staring at her over her eyeglasses until she had finished. Monsieur Dufarge began to smile, and his smile was one of great pleasure. To hear this pretty childish voice speaking his own language so simply and charmingly made him feel almost as if he were in his native land—which in dark, foggy days in London sometimes seemed worlds away. When she had finished, he took the phrase book from her, with a look similar to affection.

"Ah, madame," he said to Miss Minchin, "there is not much I can teach her. She has not learned French; she is French. Her accent is exquisite."

"You ought to have told me," she exclaimed to Sara, much mortified.

"I—I tried," said Sara. "I—I suppose I did not begin right."

Miss Minchin knew Sara had tried. And when she saw that the pupils had been listening and that Lavinia and Jessie were giggling behind their French grammars, she felt infuriated.

"Silence, young ladies!" she said severely, rapping upon the desk. "Silence at once!"

And she began from that minute to feel a grudge against her star pupil.

3

ERMENGARDE

ON THAT FIRST morning, Sara had noticed a little girl about her own age who looked at her very hard with light, rather dull blue eyes. She was a fat child who did not look in the least clever. Her flaxen hair was braided in a tight pigtail, tied with a ribbon, and she had pulled this pigtail around her neck and was biting the end of the ribbon, resting her elbows on the desk as she stared wonderingly at the new pupil. When Sara stepped forward and answered Monsieur Dufarge in French, the startled girl blushed in amazement. Having wept hopeless tears for weeks in her efforts to remember that *le mere* meant "the mother," and *le pere* meant "the father," it was almost too much to suddenly find herself listening to a child her own age who seemed not only quite familiar with these words, but knew any number of others and could mix them up with verbs as if they were mere trifles.

She stared so hard and bit the ribbon on her pigtail so fast that she attracted the attention of Miss Minchin, who, feeling extremely cross at the moment, immediately pounced upon her.

"Miss St. John!" she exclaimed severely. "What do you mean by such conduct? Remove your elbows! Take your ribbon out

24

of your mouth! Sit up at once!"

Upon which Lavinia and Jessie tittered and Miss St. John became redder than ever—so red that she looked as if tears were coming into her poor childish eyes. Sara was so sorry for her that she began rather to like her.

"If Sara had been a boy and lived a few centuries ago," her father used to say, "she would have gone about the country with her sword drawn, rescuing and defending everyone in distress. She always wants to fight when she sees people in trouble."

So she kept glancing toward fat, slow Miss St. John through the morning. She saw there was no danger of Miss St. John ever being spoiled by being treated as a star pupil. Her French lesson was a pathetic thing. Her pronunciation made even Monsieur Dufarge smile in spite of himself, and Lavinia and Jessie and the more fortunate girls either giggled or looked at her in wondering disdain. But Sara did not laugh. It made her feel savage when she heard the titters and saw the poor child's face.

"It isn't funny, really," she said between her teeth, as she bent over her book. "They ought not to laugh."

When lessons were over and the pupils gathered together in groups to talk, Sara looked for Miss St. John, and finding her bundled disconsolately in a window seat, she walked over to her and spoke.

"What is your name?" she said.

To explain Miss St. John's amazement one must recall that a new pupil with a carriage and a pony and a maid and a voyage from India was not an ordinary acquaintance.

"My name's Ermengarde St. John," she answered.

"Mine is Sara Crewe," said Sara. "Yours is very pretty. It sounds like a storybook."

"Do you like it?" fluttered Ermengarde. "I—I like yours."

Miss St. John's chief trouble in life was that she had an intellectual father. Ermengarde was a severe trial to Mr. St. John. He could not understand how a child of his could be such a dull creature who never shone in anything.

"Good heavens!" he had said more than once, as he stared at her, "there are times when I think she is as stupid as her Aunt Eliza!"

If her Aunt Eliza was slow to learn and quick to forget a thing when she had learned it, Ermengarde was strikingly like her. She was the dunce of the school, and it could not be denied.

"She must be *made* to learn," her father said to Miss Minchin.

Consequently Ermengarde spent the greater part of her life in disgrace or in tears. She learned things and forgot them, or if she remembered them, she did not understand them. So it was natural that, having met Sara, she should sit and stare at her with profound admiration.

"You can speak French, can't you?" she said respectfully.

Sara got on to the window seat, which was a big, deep one, and tucking up her feet, sat with her hands clasped round her knees.

"I can speak it because I have heard it all my life," she answered. "You could speak it if you had always heard it."

"Oh, no, I couldn't," said Ermengarde. "I never could speak it!"

"Why?" inquired Sara curiously.

Ermengarde shook her head so that the pigtail wobbled. "I can't say the words. They're so queer." She paused a moment, and then added with a touch of awe in her voice, "You are gifted, aren't you?"

Sara looked out of the window into the dingy square, where the sparrows were hopping and twittering on the wet iron railings and the sooty branches of the trees. She reflected a few moments. She had heard it said often that she was "gifted," and she wondered if she was—and if she was, how it had happened.

"I don't know," she said. "I can't tell." Then, seeing a mournful look on the round, chubby face, she gave a little laugh and changed the subject.

"Would you like to see Emily?"

"Who is Emily?" Ermengarde asked, just as Miss Minchin had done.

"Come up to my room and see," said Sara, holding out her hand.

They jumped down from the window seat together, and went upstairs.

"Is it true," Ermengarde whispered as they went through the hall, "that you have a sitting room all to yourself?"

"Yes," Sara answered. "Papa asked Miss Minchin to let me have one, because—well, it was because when I play I make up stories and tell them to myself, and I don't like people to hear me. It spoils it if I think people listen."

They had reached the passage leading to Sara's room by this time, and Ermengarde stopped short, staring, and losing her breath.

"You *make up* stories!" she gasped. "Can you do that—as well as speak French? *Can* you?"

Sara looked at her in simple surprise. "Why, anyone can make up things," she said. "Have you never tried?"

Then she put her hand warningly on Ermengarde's.

"Let us go very quietly to the door," she whispered, "and I will open it suddenly. Perhaps we may catch her."

She was half laughing, but there was a touch of mysterious hope in her eyes which fascinated Ermengarde, though she had not the remotest idea what it meant, or whom it was she wanted to "catch," or why she wanted to catch her. Whatever she meant, Ermengarde was sure it was something delightfully exciting. Thrilled with expectation, she followed on tiptoe along the passage. They made not the least noise until they reached the door. Then Sara suddenly turned the handle and threw it wide open. There was the sitting room, neat and quiet, a fire gently burning in the grate, and a wonderful doll sitting in a chair by it, apparently reading a book.

"Oh, she got back to her seat before we could see her!" Sara exclaimed. "Of course they always do. They are as quick as lightning."

Ermengarde looked from her to the doll and back again. "Can she—walk?" she asked breathlessly.

"Yes," answered Sara. "At least I believe she can. At least I *pretend* I believe she can. And that makes it seem as if it were true. Have you never pretended things?"

"No," said Ermengarde. "Never. I—tell me about it."

She was so fascinated by this odd new companion that she stared at Sara instead of at Emily—even though Emily was the most attractive doll she had ever seen.

"Let us sit down," said Sara, "and I will tell you. It's so easy that when you begin you can't stop. You just go on and on doing it always. And it's beautiful. Emily, you must listen. This is Ermengarde St. John. Ermengarde, this is Emily. Would you like to hold her?"

"Oh, may I?" said Ermengarde. "May I, really? She is beautiful!" And Emily was put into her arms.

Never in her dull, short life had Miss St. John dreamed of such an hour as the one she spent with the strange new pupil before they heard the lunch bell ring and were obliged to go downstairs.

Sara sat upon the hearth rug with her green eyes shining and her cheeks flushed. She told stories of the voyage and stories of India. But what fascinated Ermengarde most was pretending about the dolls who walked and talked and who could do anything they chose when the human beings were out of the room.

Once, when Sara was relating the story of the search for Emily, Ermengarde saw her face suddenly change. A cloud seemed to pass over it and put out the light in her shining eyes. She drew her breath in so sharply that it made a funny, sad little sound, and then she shut her lips and held them tightly closed, as if she was determined either to do or not to do something. Ermengarde had an idea that if she had been like any other little girl, she might have suddenly burst out sobbing. But she did not.

"Have you a—a pain?" Ermengarde ventured.

"Yes," Sara answered, after a moment's silence. "But it is not in my body." Then she added something in a low voice which she tried to keep steady, and it was this: "Do you love your father more than anything else in all the whole world?"

Ermengarde's mouth fell open a little. She knew it would be far from behaving like a respectable child at a select girls' school to say that it had never occurred to her that you *could* love your father, that you would do anything to avoid being left alone in his society for ten minutes. She was greatly embarrassed.

"I—I scarcely ever see him," she stammered. "He is always in the library—reading things."

"I love mine more than all the world ten times over," Sara said. "That is what my pain is. He has gone away."

She put her head quietly down on her little huddled-up knees, and sat very still for a few minutes.

She's going to cry out loud, thought Ermengarde, fearfully.

But she did not. Her short, black locks tumbled about her ears, and she sat still. Then she spoke without lifting her head.

"I promised him I would bear it," she said. "And I will. You have to bear things. Think what soldiers bear! Papa is a soldier. If there was a war he would have to bear marching and thirst and, perhaps, deep wounds. And he would never say a word—not one word."

Ermengarde could only gaze at her. Sara was wonderful and different from anyone else.

Presently she lifted her face and shook back her black locks, with a queer little smile.

"If I go on talking and talking," she said, "and telling you things about pretending, I shall bear the loneliness better."

Ermengarde did not know why a lump came into her throat and her eyes felt as if tears were in them.

"Lavinia and Jessie are 'best friends,' " Ermengarde said huskily. "Would you have me for yours? You're gifted, and I'm the stupidest girl in the school, but I—oh, I do so like you!"

"I'm glad of that," said Sara. "Yes. We will be friends. And I'll tell you what"—a sudden gleam lighting her face—"I can help you with your French lessons."

4
LOTTIE

IF SARA HAD been a different kind of child, the life she led at Miss Minchin's Select Seminary would not have been at all good for her. She was treated more as if she were a distinguished guest than as if she were a little girl. Privately Miss Minchin disliked her, but she knew that if Sara wrote to her papa to tell him she was uncomfortable or unhappy, Captain Crewe would remove her at once. Accordingly, Sara was praised for her quickness at her lessons, for her good manners, for her friendliness to her fellow pupils, for her generosity if she gave sixpence to a beggar out of her full little purse. The simplest thing she did was treated as if it were a virtue, and if she had not had a clever little brain, she might have been self-satisfied. But the clever little brain told her a great many sensible and true things about herself, and now and then she talked these things over with Ermengarde.

"Things happen to people by accident," she used to say. "A lot of nice accidents have happened to me. It just happened that I always liked lessons and books and could remember things when I learned them. It just happened that I was born with a nice father who could give me everything I liked. If you have everything you want and everyone is kind to you, how can you help but be good-tempered? I don't know"—looking quite serious—"how I shall ever find out whether I am really a nice child. Perhaps I'm a horrid child, and no one will ever know, just because I never have any trials."

"Lavinia has no trials," said Ermengarde without emotion, "and she is horrid enough."

Sara rubbed the end of her little nose as she thought the matter over.

"Well," she said at last, "perhaps—perhaps that is because Lavinia is growing." She had heard Miss Amelia say that Lavinia was growing so fast that she believed it affected her health and temper.

Lavinia, in fact, was jealous of Sara. She used to be the leader in the school because she was capable of making herself extremely disagreeable if the others did not follow her. She was pretty and had been the best-dressed pupil in the procession when the pupils walked out two by two, until Sara's velvet coats and sable muffs appeared, combined with drooping ostrich feathers, and Miss Minchin put her at the head of the line. This had been bitter enough, but as time went on it became apparent that Sara was a leader, not because she could make herself disagreeable, but because she never did.

"There's one thing about Sara Crewe," Jessie had enraged her best friend by saying honestly, "she's never 'grand' about herself the least bit, and you know she might be, Lavvie. I believe I couldn't help being—just a little—if I had so many fine things and was made such a fuss over. It's disgusting, the way Miss Minchin shows her off when parents come."

" 'Dear Sara must come into the drawing room and talk to Mrs. Musgrave about India,' " mimicked Lavinia, in her most highly flavored imitation of Miss Minchin. " 'Dear Sara must speak French to Lady Pitkin. Her accent is so perfect.' She didn't learn her French here, and there's nothing so clever in her knowing it. She says herself she didn't learn it at all. She just picked it up, because she always heard her papa speak it. And as to her papa, there is nothing so grand in being an army officer in India."

"Well," said Jessie, slowly, "he's killed tigers. He killed the one in the skin Sara has in her room. That's why she likes it so. She lies on it and strokes its head, and talks to it as if it was a cat."

"She's always doing something silly," snapped Lavinia. "My mamma says she will grow up eccentric."

It was true that Sara was never "grand." The little ones, who were accustomed to being disdained and ordered out of the way by mature ladies aged ten and twelve, were never made to cry by Sara. She was a motherly young person. When people fell down and scraped their knees, she ran and helped them up and patted them, or found in her pocket a piece of candy or some other soothing item. She never pushed them out of her way or alluded to their age as a humiliation and a blot upon their small characters.

"If she is four she is four," Sara said severely to Lavinia, who had slapped Lottie and called her a brat. "But she will be five next year, and six the year after that. And," opening large, convicting eyes, "it takes sixteen years to make her twenty."

"Dear me," said Lavinia, "how we can calculate!"

So the younger children adored Sara. More than once she had been known to have a tea party, made up of these despised ones, in her own room. And Emily had been played with and Emily's own tea service used—the one with cups that held quite a lot of much-sweetened weak tea and had blue flowers on them. No one had seen such a doll's tea set before. From that afternoon Sara was regarded as a goddess and a queen by the entire beginners class.

Lottie Legh worshiped her. Lottie had been sent to school by a flighty young papa who could not imagine what else to do with her. Her young mother had died, and as Lottie had been treated like a favorite doll or a spoiled pet ever since the first hour of her life, she was an appalling little creature. When she wanted anything or did not want anything she wept and howled; and as she always wanted the things she could not have and did not want the things that were best for her, her shrill little voice was usually heard wailing in one part of the house or another.

She had found out that a very small girl who had lost her mother ought to be pitied, and she made great use of this knowledge.

One morning Sara heard both Miss Minchin and Miss Amelia trying to suppress Lottie's angry wails in a closed room.

"What *is* she crying for?" Miss Minchin almost yelled.

"Oh—oh—oh!" Sara heard. "I haven't got any mam—ma-a!"

"Oh, Lottie!" screamed Miss Amelia. "Do stop, darling! Don't cry! Please don't!"

"Oh! Oh!" Lottie howled. "Haven't—got—any—mam—ma-a!"

"She ought to be whipped," Miss Minchin proclaimed. "You *shall* be whipped, you naughty child!"

Lottie wailed more loudly than ever. Miss Amelia began to cry. Miss Minchin's voice rose until it almost thundered, then suddenly she sprang up from her chair in indignation and left the room, leaving Miss Amelia to settle the matter.

Sara had paused in the hall, and when Miss Minchin came out and saw her, she realized that her voice could not have sounded either dignified or amiable.

"Oh, Sara!" she exclaimed, endeavoring to produce a suitable smile.

"I stopped," explained Sara, "because I knew it was Lottie—and I thought, perhaps—just perhaps, I could make her be quiet. May I try, Miss Minchin?"

"If you can, you are a clever child," answered Miss Minchin, much annoyed. Then seeing that Sara looked slightly chilled, she changed her manner. "But you are clever in everything," she said in her approving way. "I dare say you can manage her. Go in." And she left.

When Sara entered the room, Lottie was lying upon the floor, screaming and kicking her small fat legs violently, and poor plump Miss Amelia was bending over her in alarm and despair, looking quite red and damp with heat, trying first one method and then another.

"Poor darling," she said one moment, "I know you haven't any mamma, poor—" Then in quite another tone, "If you don't stop, Lottie, I will shake you. Poor little angel! There—! You wicked, bad, detestable child, I will smack you! I will!"

Sara did not know at all what she was going to do, but she had a vague conviction that it would be better not to say such different kinds of things so helplessly and excitedly.

"Miss Amelia," she said in a low voice, "Miss Minchin says I may try to make her stop. May I?"

Miss Amelia turned and looked at her hopelessly. "Oh, do you think you can?" she gasped.

"I don't know whether I can," answered Sara, still in her half-whisper, "but I will try."

Miss Amelia stumbled up from her knees with a heavy sigh, and Lottie's fat little legs kicked as hard as ever.

"If you will steal out of the room," said Sara, "I will stay with her."

"Oh, Sara!" whimpered Miss Amelia. "We never had such a dreadful child before." But she crept out of the room and was much relieved to find an excuse for doing it.

Sara stood by the howling child for a few moments, and looked down at her without saying anything. Then she sat down on the floor beside her and waited. Except for Lottie's angry screams, the room was quiet. This was a new state of affairs for little Miss Legh, who was accustomed, when she screamed, to hear other people protest and implore and command and coax by turns. To lie and kick and shriek, and find the only person near you not seeming to mind in the least, attracted her attention. She opened her tight-shut streaming eyes to see who this person was. It was the girl who owned Emily and all the nice things. Having paused for a few seconds to find this out, Lottie thought she must begin again, but the quiet of the room and Sara's odd, interested face made her howl half-hearted.

"I—haven't—any—mam—ma-a!" she announced, but her voice was not so strong.

Sara looked at her with understanding in her eyes.

"Neither have I," she said.

This was so unexpected that it was astounding. Lottie dropped her legs, gave a wriggle, and lay and stared. A new idea will stop a crying child when nothing else will. Also it was true that while Lottie disliked Miss Minchin, who was cross, and Miss Amelia, who was foolish, she liked Sara, little as she knew her. She did not want to give up her grievance, but after a sulky sob she said, "Where is she?"

Sara paused a moment. Because she had been told that her mamma was in heaven, she had thought a great deal about the matter, and her thoughts had not been quite like those of other people.

"She went to heaven," she said. "But I am sure she comes out sometimes to see me—though I don't see her. So does yours.

Perhaps they can both see us now. Perhaps they are both in this room."

Lottie sat bolt upright and looked about her. She was a pretty little curly-headed creature, and her round eyes were like wet forget-me-nots.

Sara went on talking. Perhaps some people might think that what she said was like a fairy story, but it was all so real to her own imagination that Lottie began to listen in spite of herself. Lottie had been told that her mamma had wings and a crown, and she had been shown pictures of ladies in beautiful white nightgowns. But Sara seemed to be telling a real story about a lovely country where real people were.

"There are fields and fields of flowers," she said, talking as if she were in a dream, "fields and fields of lilies—and when the soft wind blows over them it wafts the scent of them into the air—and everybody always breathes it, because the soft wind is always blowing. And little children run about in the lily fields and gather armfuls of them, and laugh and make little wreaths. And the streets are shining. And people are never tired, however far they walk. They can float anywhere they like. And there are walls made of pearl and gold all round the city, but they are low enough for the people to go and lean on them, and look down on the earth and smile, and send beautiful messages."

Lottie dragged herself close to Sara and drank in every word until the end came—far too soon. When it did come, she was so sorry that she stuck out her lip.

"I want to go there," she cried. "I—haven't any mamma in this school."

Sara saw the danger signal and came out of her dream. She took hold of the chubby hand and pulled Lottie close to her side with a coaxing little laugh.

"I will be your mamma," she said. "We will play that you are my little girl. And Emily shall be your sister."

Lottie's dimples all began to show themselves.

"Shall she?" she said.

"Yes," answered Sara, jumping to her feet. "Let us go and tell her. And then I will wash your face and brush your hair."

To which Lottie agreed cheerfully, and trotted out of the room and upstairs with her, without seeming to remember that the last hour's tragedy had been caused by her refusal to be washed and brushed for lunch.

And from that time Sara was an adopted mother.

5
BECKY

OF COURSE WHAT gained Sara even more followers than her luxuries and the fact that she was "the star pupil" was her power of telling stories and of making everything she talked about seem like a story.

Sara not only could tell stories, but she adored telling them. When she began to invent wonderful things, her green eyes grew big and shining, her cheeks flushed, and without knowing that she was doing it, she made what she told lovely or alarming by the raising or dropping of her voice, the bend and sway of her slim body, and the dramatic movement of her hands. She saw and lived with the fairy folk or the kings and queens and beautiful ladies whose adventures she was narrating. Sometimes when she had finished her story, she was out of breath with excitement and would lay her hand on her thin little quick-rising chest and half laugh at herself.

"When I am telling it," she would say, "it doesn't seem as if it was only made up. It seems more real than the schoolroom. I feel as if I were all the people in the story—one after the other. It is strange."

She had been at Miss Minchin's school about two years when one foggy winter's afternoon—as she was getting out of her carriage comfortably wrapped up in her warmest velvets and furs and looking grander than she knew—she caught sight, as she crossed the pavement, of a dingy little figure standing on the steps and stretching its neck so that its wide-open eyes might peer at her through the railings. She smiled because it was her way to smile at people.

But the owner of the smudgy face and the wide-open eyes evidently was afraid that she ought not to have been caught looking. She dodged out of sight like a jack-in-the-box and scurried back into the kitchen, disappearing so suddenly that if she had not been such a poor little forlorn thing, Sara would have laughed. That evening, as Sara was sitting in the midst of a group of listeners in a corner of the schoolroom telling one of her stories, the very same figure timidly entered the room, carrying a coal box much too heavy for her, and knelt down upon the hearth rug to replenish the fire and sweep up the ashes.

She was evidently afraid to look at the children or seem to be listening. She put on pieces of coal cautiously with her fingers so that she might make no disturbing noise, and she swept about the fire irons very softly. But Sara saw in two minutes that she was deeply interested in what was going on, and that she was doing her work slowly in the hope of catching a word here and there. Realizing this, Sara raised her voice and spoke more clearly.

"The Mermaids swam softly about in the crystal-green water, and dragged after them a fishing-net woven of deep-sea pearls," she said. "The Princess sat on the white rock and watched them."

It was a wonderful story about a princess who was loved by a Prince Merman and went to live with him in shining caves under the sea.

The small drudge before the grate swept the hearth once

and then swept it again. As she was doing it the third time, the sound of the story so lured her to listen that she fell under the spell and forgot that she had no right to listen at all, and also forgot everything else. The voice of the storyteller went on and drew her with it into winding grottoes under the sea, glowing with soft, clear blue light, and paved with pure golden sands. Strange sea flowers and grasses waved about her, and far away faint singing and music echoed.

The idle hearth brush fell from the work-roughened hand, and Lavinia Herbert looked round.

"That girl has been listening," she said.

The culprit snatched up her brush and scrambled to her feet. She caught at the coal box and scuttled out of the room like a frightened rabbit.

Sara felt rather hot-tempered.

"I knew she was listening," she said. "Why shouldn't she?"

Lavinia tossed her head with great elegance.

"Well," she remarked, "I do not know whether your mamma would like you to tell stories to servant girls, but I know *my* mamma wouldn't like *me* to do it."

"My mamma?" said Sara, looking odd. "I don't believe she would mind in the least. She knows that stories belong to everybody."

"I thought," retorted Lavinia, "that your mamma was dead. How can she know things?"

"Do you think she *doesn't* know things?" said Sara, in her stern little voice.

"Sara's mamma knows everything," piped in Lottie. "The streets are shining, and there are fields and fields of lilies, and everybody gathers them. Sara tells me when she puts me to bed."

"You wicked thing," said Lavinia, turning on Sara, "making fairy stories about heaven."

"There are much more splendid stories in the book of Revelation," returned Sara. "Just look and see! How do you know mine are fairy stories? But I can tell you"—with a fine bit of unheavenly temper—"you will never find out whether they are or not if you're not kinder to people than you are now. Come along, Lottie." And she marched out of the room.

"Who is that little girl who makes the fires?" she asked Mariette that night.

Mariette broke forth into a flow of description. Ah, indeed, Mademoiselle Sara might well ask. She was the new *scullery maid—though she was everything else besides. She blacked boots and grates, and carried heavy coal-scuttles up and down stairs, and scrubbed floors, and cleaned windows, and was ordered about by everybody. She was fourteen years old, but was so stunted in growth that she looked about twelve. In truth, Mariette was sorry for her. She was so timid that if one chanced to speak to her it appeared as if her poor, frightened eyes would jump out of her head.

"What is her name?" asked Sara.

Her name was Becky. Mariette heard everyone downstairs calling, "Becky, do this," and "Becky, do that," every five minutes in the day.

Sara sat and looked into the fire, reflecting on Becky for some time after Mariette left her. She thought she looked as if she had never had enough to eat. Her very eyes were hungry. She hoped she should see her again, but though she caught sight of her carrying things up or down stairs on several occasions, she always seemed in such a hurry and so afraid of being seen that it was impossible to speak to her.

But a few weeks later, on another foggy afternoon, when Sara

---

*scullery: a room near the kitchen for washing and storing dishes and preparing vegetables.

entered her sitting room she found Becky in her own special easy chair before the bright fire. With a coal smudge on her nose and several on her apron, with her poor little cap hanging half off her head, and an empty coal box on the floor near her—Becky sat fast asleep, tired out beyond even the endurance of her hard-working young body. She had been sent up to put the bedrooms in order for the evening. There were a great many of them, and she had been running about all day. Sara's rooms were not like the other rooms, which were plain and bare. This comfortable sitting room seemed a bower of luxury to the scullery maid, though it was, in fact, merely a nice, bright little room. But there were pictures and books in it and curious things from India; there was a sofa and the low, soft chair. Becky saved this room until the end of her afternoon's work, because it rested her to go into it, and she always hoped to snatch a few minutes to sit down in the soft chair and look about her, and think about the wonderful good fortune of the child who lived there.

When she had sat down this afternoon, the relief to her short, aching legs had been so wonderful and delightful that it had seemed to soothe her whole body, and the glow of warmth and comfort from the fire had crept over her like a spell, until, as she looked at the red coals, a tired, slow smile stole over her smudged face, her head nodded forward without her being aware of it, her eyes drooped, and she fell fast asleep. She had been there only about ten minutes when Sara entered, but she was in as deep a sleep as if she had been, like Sleeping Beauty, slumbering for a hundred years. But she did not look like a Sleeping Beauty at all. She looked only like a stunted, worn-out little scullery drudge.

Sara seemed as much unlike her as if she were a creature from another world.

Sara had been taking her dancing lesson, and the afternoon on which the dancing master appeared every week was a grand occasion. The pupils were dressed in their prettiest frocks, and as Sara danced particularly well, Mariette was requested to make her as elegant and refined as possible.

Today a frock the color of a rose had been put on her, and Mariette had bought some real buds and made her a wreath to wear on her black locks. She had been learning a delightful dance in which she had been skimming and flying about the room like a large rose-colored butterfly, and the enjoyment and exercise had brought a brilliant, happy glow to her face.

When she entered the room, she floated in with a few of the butterfly steps—and there sat Becky, nodding her cap sideways off her head.

"Oh!" cried Sara, softly, when she saw her. "That poor thing!" She crept toward her quietly and stood looking. Becky gave a little snore.

"I wish she'd waken herself," Sara said. "I don't like to waken her. But Miss Minchin would be cross if she found out. I'll just wait a few minutes."

She took a seat on the edge of the table and sat swinging her slim, rose-colored legs and wondering what it would be best to do. Miss Amelia might come in at any moment, and if she did Becky would be sure to be scolded.

"But she is so tired," she thought. "She is so tired!"

A piece of flaming coal ended her perplexity that very moment. It broke off from a large lump and fell on to the fender. Becky started and opened her eyes with a frightened gasp. She did not know she had fallen asleep. She had only sat down for one moment and felt the beautiful glow—and here she found herself staring in wild alarm at the wonderful girl who sat perched near her, like a rose-colored fairy with interested eyes.

44

"She is so tired!"

She sprang up and clutched at her cap. She felt it dangling over her ear, and tried wildly to put it straight. Oh, she had got herself into trouble now with a vengeance! To have rudely fallen asleep on such a young lady's chair! She would be turned out of doors without wages.

She made a sound like a big breathless sob.

"Oh, miss! Oh, miss!" she stuttered. "I arst yer pardon, miss! Oh, I do, miss!"

Sara jumped down and came close to her.

"Don't be frightened," she said, as if she had been speaking to a little girl like herself. "It doesn't matter the least bit."

"I didn't go to do it, miss," protested Becky. "It was the warm fire—an' me bein' so tired. It—it wasn't impertence!"

Sara broke into a friendly little laugh and put her hand on her shoulder.

"You were tired," she said. "You could not help it. You are not really awake yet."

How poor Becky stared at her! She had never heard such a nice, friendly sound in anyone's voice before. She was used to being ordered about and scolded and having her ears boxed. But this girl in the rose-colored dancing splendor was looking at her as if she were not a culprit at all—as if she had a right to be tired—even to fall asleep! The touch of the soft, slim little hand on her shoulder was the most amazing thing she had ever known.

"Ain't—ain't yer angry, miss?" she gasped. "Ain't yer goin to tell the missus?"

"No," cried out Sara. "Of course I'm not." The woeful fright in the coal-smutted face made one of Sara's queer thoughts rush into her mind. She put her hand against Becky's cheek.

"Why," she said, "we are just the same—I am only a little girl like you. It's just an accident that I am not you, and you are not me!"

Becky did not understand in the least. Her mind could not grasp such amazing thoughts, and "an accident" meant to her a calamity in which someone was run over or fell off a ladder and was carried to "the 'orspital."

"A' accident, miss," she fluttered respectfully. "Is it?"

"Yes," Sara answered, and she looked at her dreamily for a moment. But the next she spoke in a different tone.

"Have you finished your work?" she asked. "Dare you stay here a few minutes?"

Becky lost her breath again.

"Here, miss? Me?"

Sara ran to the door, opened it, and looked out and listened.

"No one is anywhere about," she explained. "If your bedrooms are finished, perhaps you might stay a tiny while. I thought—perhaps—you might like a piece of cake."

The next ten minutes seemed to Becky like a sort of delirium. Sara opened a cupboard and gave her a thick slice of cake. She seemed to rejoice when it was devoured in hungry bites. She talked and asked questions, and laughed until Becky's fears actually began to calm themselves.

"Is that—" Becky ventured, looking longingly at the rose-colored frock. And she asked it almost in a whisper. "Is that there your best?"

"It is one of my dancing frocks," answered Sara. "I like it, don't you?"

For a few seconds Becky was almost speechless with admiration. Then she said in an awed voice, "Oncet I see a princess. I was standin' in the street with the crowd outside Covin' Garden, watchin' the swells go inter the op'ra. An' there was one pink all over everyone stared at. They says to each other,

'That's the princess.' You look like her."

"I've often thought," said Sara, in her reflecting voice, "that I should like to be a princess. I believe I will begin pretending I am one."

Becky stared at her admiringly, and, as before, did not understand her in the least. She watched her with a sort of adoration. Soon Sara turned to her with a new question.

"Becky," she said, "weren't you listening to that story?"

"Yes, miss," confessed Becky, a little alarmed again. "I knowed I hadn't orter, but it was that beautiful I—I couldn't help it."

"I liked you to listen to it," said Sara. "If you tell stories, you like nothing so much as to tell them to people who want to listen. Would you like to hear the rest?"

Becky lost her breath again.

"Me hear it?" she cried. "Like as if I was a pupil, miss? All about the Prince—and the little white Mer-babies swimming about laughing—with stars in their hair?"

Sara nodded.

"You haven't time to hear it now, I'm afraid," she said, "but if you will tell me just what time you come to do my rooms, I will try to be here and tell you a bit of it every day until it is finished. It's a lovely long one—and I'm always putting new bits to it."

"Then," breathed Becky, devoutly, "I wouldn't mind how heavy the coal boxes was—or *what* the cook done to me, if—if I might have that to think of."

"You may," said Sara. "I'll tell it all to you."

When Becky went downstairs, she was not the same Becky who had staggered up, loaded down by the weight of the coal scuttle. She had an extra piece of cake in her pocket, and she had been fed and warmed by cake and fire. But something else had warmed and fed her, and the something else was Sara.

48

When Becky was gone Sara sat on her favorite perch on the end of her table. Her feet were on a chair, her elbows on her knees, and her chin in her hands.

"If I was a princess—a real princess," she murmured, "I could scatter my wealth to the populace. But even if I am only a pretend princess, I can invent little things to do for people. Things like this."

6

THE DIAMOND MINES

NOT LONG AFTER this an exciting thing happened that became the chief subject of school conversation for weeks. In one of his letters Captain Crewe told about a friend who had been at school with him when he was a boy coming unexpectedly to see him in India. This friend owned a large tract of land upon which diamonds had been found, and if all went as expected he would possess such wealth as it made one dizzy to think of; and he gave Sara's father an opportunity to share in this enormous fortune by becoming a partner. "Diamond mines" sounded so like the *Arabian Nights* that Sara thought them enchanting, and for Ermengarde and Lottie she described tunnels underground where sparkling stones studded the walls and roofs and ceilings, and dark men dug them out with heavy picks. Ermengarde delighted in the story, and Lottie insisted on its being retold to her every evening. Lavinia was spiteful about it and told Jessie that she didn't believe such things as diamond mines existed.

"My mamma has a diamond ring which cost forty pounds," she said. "And it is not a big one, either. If there were mines full of diamonds, people would be so rich it would be ridiculous."

"Perhaps Sara will be so rich that she will be ridiculous," giggled Jessie.

"She's ridiculous without being rich," Lavinia sniffed.

"I believe you hate her," said Jessie.

"No, I don't," snapped Lavinia. "But I don't believe in mines full of diamonds."

"Well, people have to get them from somewhere," said Jessie. Then she giggled, "Lavinia, what do you think Gertrude says?"

"I don't know, I'm sure. And I don't care, if it's about Sara."

"Well, it is. One of her 'pretends' is that she is a princess. She plays it all the time—even in school. She wants Ermengarde to be one, too, but Ermengarde says she is too fat."

"She *is* too fat," said Lavinia. "And Sara is too thin."

Jessie giggled. "She says it has nothing to do with what you look like or what you have. It has only to do with what you think of and what you do."

"I suppose she thinks she could be a princess if she was a beggar," said Lavinia. "Let us begin to call her 'your royal highness.' "

Lessons for the day were over, and they were sitting before the schoolroom fire, enjoying the time they liked best. It was the time when Miss Minchin and Miss Amelia were taking their tea in the small sitting room sacred to themselves. At this hour a great deal of talking was done, and a great many secrets changed hands, particularly if the younger pupils behaved themselves well and did not squabble or run about noisily, which they usually did. The older girls were expected to keep order, and there was danger that if they did not, Miss Minchin or Miss Amelia would appear and send them out of the schoolroom. Even as Lavinia spoke, the door opened and Sara entered with Lottie, whose habit was to trot everywhere after her like a little dog.

"There she is, with that horrid child!" exclaimed Lavinia in a whisper. "She will begin howling about something in five minutes."

It happened that Lottie had been seized with a sudden desire to play in the schoolroom and had begged Sara to come. Sara curled herself up in the window seat and opened a book about the French Revolution. She was soon lost in a harrowing picture of the prisoners in the Bastille—men who had spent so many years in dungeons that when they were dragged out by those who rescued them, their long, gray hair and beards almost hid their faces. The men had forgotten that an outside world existed at all, and were like beings in a dream.

She was dragged back suddenly by a howl from Lottie. Never did she find anything so difficult as to keep herself from losing her temper when she was suddenly disturbed while absorbed in a book.

"It makes me feel as if someone had hit me," Sara had told Ermengarde once in confidence. "And as if I want to hit back. I have to remember things quickly to keep from saying something ill-tempered." She had to remember things quickly now when she laid her book on the window seat and jumped down from her comfortable corner.

Lottie had been sliding across the schoolroom floor and had ended by falling down and hurting her fat knee. She was screaming and dancing up and down in the midst of a group of friends and enemies who were alternately coaxing and scolding her.

"Stop this minute, you crybaby! Stop this minute!" Lavinia commanded.

"I'm not a crybaby . . . I'm not!" wailed Lottie. "Sara, Sa—ra!"

"If she doesn't stop, Miss Minchin will hear her," cried Jessie. "Lottie darling, I'll give you a penny!"

"I don't want your penny," sobbed Lottie. She looked down at the fat knee, and seeing a drop of blood on it, burst forth again.

Sara flew across the room and, kneeling down, put her arms round her.

"Now, Lottie," she said. "Now, Lottie, you *promised* Sara."

"She said I was a crybaby," wept Lottie.

Sara patted her, but spoke in the steady voice Lottie knew.

"But if you cry, you will be one, Lottie pet. You *promised.*"

Lottie remembered that she had promised, but she preferred to lift up her voice.

"I haven't any mamma," she proclaimed.

"Yes, you have," said Sara, cheerfully. "Have you forgotten? Don't you know that Sara is your mamma? Don't you want Sara for your mamma?"

Lottie cuddled up to her with a consoled sniff.

"Come and sit in the window seat with me," Sara went on, "and I'll whisper a story to you."

"Will you?" whimpered Lottie. "Will you tell me about the diamond mines?"

"The diamond mines?" broke out Lavinia. "Nasty little spoiled thing, I should like to *slap* her!"

Sara got up quickly on her feet. She was not an angel, and she was not fond of Lavinia.

"Well," she said, with some fire, "I should like to slap *you*—but I don't want to slap you!" restraining herself. "At least I both want to slap you—and I should like to slap you—but I *won't* slap you. We are not little gutter children."

Here was Lavinia's opportunity.

"Ah, yes, your royal highness," she said. "We are princesses, I believe. At least one of us is. The school ought to be very fashionable now that Miss Minchin has a princess for a pupil."

Sara started toward her. She looked as if she were going to box her ears. Perhaps she was. Her new "pretend" about being a princess was very near to her heart, and she was shy and sensitive about it. She had meant it to be a secret, and here was Lavinia making fun of it before nearly all the school. She felt the blood rush up into her face and tingle in her ears. She only just saved herself. If you were a princess, you did not fly into rages. Her hand dropped, and she stood still a moment. When she spoke it was in a quiet, steady voice.

"It's true," she said. "Sometimes I do pretend I am a princess. I pretend I am a princess so that I can try and behave like one."

Lavinia could invent only one remark, and it fell flat. "Dear me," she said, "I hope, when you ascend the throne, you won't forget us!"

"I won't," said Sara, and she did not utter another word, but stood still and stared while Lavinia took Jessie's arm and turned away.

After this, the girls who were jealous of her used to speak of her as "Princess Sara" whenever they wished to be disdainful, and those who were fond of her gave her the name among themselves as a term of affection.

To Becky it seemed the most appropriate thing in the world. The acquaintance begun on the foggy afternoon when she had jumped up terrified from her sleep had ripened and grown. Miss Minchin and Miss Amelia were aware that Sara was "kind" to the scullery maid, but they knew nothing of certain delightful moments snatched perilously in Sara's sitting room, when the heavy coal box was set down with a sigh of joy. At such times stories were told by installments, and things were either eaten there or hastily tucked into pockets to be eaten at night when Becky went upstairs to her attic to bed.

"But I has to eat 'em careful, miss," she said once, " 'cos if I leaves crumbs the rats come out to get 'em."

"Rats!" exclaimed Sara, in horror. "Are there *rats* there?"

"Lots of 'em, miss," Becky answered in a matter-of-fact manner. "There mostly is rats an' mice in attics. You gets used to the noise they makes scuttling about. I've got so I don't mind 'em 's long as they don't run over my piller."

"Ugh!" said Sara.

"You gets used to anythin' after a bit," said Becky. "You have to, miss, if you're born a scullery maid. I'd rather have rats than cockroaches."

"So would I," said Sara. "I suppose you might make friends with a rat in time, but I don't believe I should like to make friends with a cockroach."

Sometimes Becky did not dare to spend more than a few minutes in the bright, warm room, and when this was the case only a few words could be exchanged and a small purchase slipped into the old-fashioned pocket Becky carried under her skirt, tied around her waist. Providing small packets of food for Becky added a new interest to Sara's existence. When she drove or walked out, she used to look into shop windows eagerly. The first time it occurred to her to bring home two or three little meat pies, Becky's eyes sparkled.

"Oh, miss!" she murmured. "Them will be nice an' fillin'. It's fillin'ness that's best. Sponge cake's a 'eavenly thing, but it melts away like, if you understand, miss. These'll just *stay* in yer stummick."

They were filling—and so were beef sandwiches, bought at a cook-shop, and so were rolls and bologna sausage. In time, Becky began to lose her hungry, tired feeling, and the coal box did not seem so unbearably heavy.

However heavy it was, and whatever the temper of the cook

and the hardness of the work heaped upon her shoulders, she always looked forward to the chance that Miss Sara would be in her sitting room that afternoon. In fact, the mere seeing of Miss Sara would have been enough without meat pies. If there was time only for a few words, they were always friendly, merry words that put heart into one. Sara—who was only doing what she unconsciously liked better than anything else, God having made her for a giver—had not the least idea what she meant to poor Becky and how wonderful a benefactor she seemed. If God has made you to be a giver, your hands are born open and so is your heart. And, though there may be times when your hands are empty, your heart is always full and you can give things out of that—warm things, kind things, sweet things, help and comfort and laughter. Sometimes gay, kind laughter is the best help of all.

Becky had scarcely known what laughter was through all her poor little hard-driven life. Sara made her laugh and laughed with her, and though neither of them knew it, the laughter was as "fillin'" as the meat pies.

A few weeks before Sara's eleventh birthday a letter came to her from her father, which did not seem to be written in such boyish high spirits as usual. He was not well and was evidently burdened by the business connected with the diamond mines.

"You see, little Sara," he wrote, "your daddy is not a businessman at all, and figures and documents bother him. He does not really understand them, and all this seems so enormous. Perhaps if I was not feverish I should not be awake, tossing about one half of the night and spending the other half in troublesome dreams. If my little missus were here, I dare say she would give me some solemn, good advice. You would, wouldn't you, Little Missus?"

One of his many jokes had been to call her his "little missus" because she had such an old-fashioned air.

He had made wonderful preparations for her birthday. Among other things, a new doll had been ordered in Paris, and her wardrobe was to be splendid. When Sara had replied to his letter asking her if the doll would be an acceptable present, she had been very quaint.

"I am getting old," she wrote. "This will be my last doll. There is something solemn about it. If I could write poetry, I am sure a poem about 'A Last Doll' would be very nice. But I cannot write poetry. I have tried, and it made me laugh. It did not sound like Watts or Coleridge or Shakespeare at all. No one could ever take Emily's place, but I should respect the Last Doll very much; and I am sure the school would love it. They all like dolls, though some of the big girls—the almost fifteen ones—pretend they are too grown up."

Captain Crewe had a splitting headache when he read this letter in his bungalow in India. The table before him was heaped with papers and letters which were alarming him and filling him with anxious dread, but he laughed as he had not laughed for weeks.

"Oh," he said, "she's better fun every year she lives. God grant this business may right itself and leave me free to run home and see her. What wouldn't I give to have her little arms round my neck this minute! What *wouldn't* I give!"

The birthday was to be celebrated by great festivities. The boxes containing the presents were to be opened with great ceremony, and there was to be a glittering feast spread in Miss Minchin's sacred room. When the day arrived the whole house was in a whirl of excitement. How the morning passed nobody knew, because there seemed such preparations to be made. The schoolroom was being decked with garlands of holly, and the desks had been moved away.

When Sara went into her sitting room in the morning, she found on the table a small, dumpy package tied up in a piece of brown paper. She knew it was a present, and she thought she could guess whom it came from. She opened it tenderly. It was a square pincushion, made of not quite clean red flannel, and black pins had been stuck carefully into it to form the words, "Menny hapy returns."

"Oh!" cried Sara, with a warm feeling in her heart. "What pains she has taken! I like it so, it—it makes me feel sorrowful."

But the next moment she was mystified. On the under side of the pincushion was a card bearing in neat letters the name "Miss Amelia Minchin."

Sara turned it over and over.

"Miss Amelia!" she said to herself. "How *can* it be!"

Just at that moment she heard the door being cautiously pushed open and saw Becky peeping round it.

There was an affectionate, happy grin on her face, and she shuffled forward and stood nervously pulling at her fingers.

"Do yer like it, Miss Sara?" she said. "Do yer?"

"Like it?" cried Sara. "You darling Becky, you made it all yourself."

Becky's eyes were moist with delight.

"It ain't nothin but flannin, an' the flannin ain't new; but I wanted to give yer somethin' an' I made it of nights. I knew yer could pretend it was satin with diamond pins in. I tried to when I was makin' it. The card, miss," she said rather doubtfully, " 'twarn't wrong of me to pick it up out o' the dust-bin, was it? Miss 'Meliar had throwed it away. I hadn't no card o' my own, an' I knowed it wouldn't be a proper presink if I didn't pin a card on—so I pinned Miss 'Meliar's."

Sara flew at her and hugged her. She could not have told

herself or anyone else why there was a lump in her throat.

"Oh, Becky!" she cried out, with a queer little laugh, "I love you, Becky—I do, I do!"

"Oh, miss!" breathed Becky. "Thank yer, miss, kindly. It ain't good enough for that. The—the flannin wasn't new."

7

THE DIAMOND MINES AGAIN

WHEN SARA ENTERED the holly-hung schoolroom in the afternoon, she was at the head of a procession. Miss Minchin, in her grandest silk dress, led Sara by the hand. A manservant followed, carrying the box containing the Last Doll; a housemaid carried a second box; and Becky brought up the rear, carrying a third and wearing a clean apron and a new cap. Miss Minchin had insisted on this grand entry.

"This is not an ordinary occasion," she told Sara in advance. "Silence, young ladies!" she said to the girls. "James, place the box on the table and remove the lid. Emma, put yours upon a chair. Becky!"

Becky was so excited that she had been grinning at Lottie, who was wriggling with expectation. Becky's frightened, bobbing curtsy of apology was so funny that Lavinia and Jessie tittered.

"It is not your place to look at the young ladies," said Miss Minchin. "Put your box down. You may leave."

Becky obeyed and hastily backed toward the door. She could not help casting a longing glance at the box on the table. Something made of blue satin was peeping from between the folds of tissue paper.

"If you please, Miss Minchin," said Sara suddenly, "mayn't Becky stay?"

It was a bold thing to do. Miss Minchin put her eyeglass up and gazed at her star pupil disturbedly.

"Becky?" she exclaimed. "My dearest Sara!"

Sara advanced a step toward her.

"I want her because I know she will like to see the presents," she explained. "She is a little girl too, you know."

Miss Minchin was scandalized. She glanced from one figure to the other.

"My dear Sara," she said, "Becky is the scullery maid. Scullery maids—er—are not little girls."

To her, scullery maids were machines who carried coal scuttles and made fires.

"But Becky is," said Sara. "And I know she would enjoy herself. Please let her stay—because it is my birthday."

Miss Minchin replied with much dignity: "As a birthday favor—she may stay. Rebecca, thank Miss Sara for her great kindness."

Becky had been backing into the corner, twisting the hem of her apron in suspense. She came forward, bobbing curtsies, but between Sara's eyes and her own there passed a gleam of friendly understanding, while her words tumbled over each other.

"Oh, if you please, miss! I'm that grateful, miss! I did want to see the doll, miss, that I did. Thank you, miss. And thank you, ma'am," turning and making an alarmed bob to Miss Minchin, "for letting me take the liberty."

Miss Minchin waved her hand in the direction of the corner near the door. "Go and stand there," she commanded. "Not too near the young ladies."

Becky did not care where she was sent, so long as she was

inside the room instead of being downstairs in the scullery while these delights were going on.

"Now, young ladies, I have a few words to say to you," Miss Minchin announced.

"She's going to make a speech," whispered one of the girls. "I wish it was over."

"You are aware, young ladies," the speech began, "that dear Sara is eleven years old today."

"*Dear* Sara!" murmured Lavinia.

"Several of you here have also been eleven years old, but Sara's birthdays are rather different from other little girls' birthdays. When she is older she will be heiress to a large fortune which it will be her duty to spend wisely."

"The diamond mines," giggled Jessie, in a whisper.

"When her dear papa, Captain Crewe, brought her from India and gave her into my care, he said to me, in a jesting way, 'I am afraid she will be very rich, Miss Minchin.' My reply was, 'Her education at my seminary, Captain Crewe, shall be such as will adorn the largest fortune.' Sara has become my most accomplished pupil. Her French and her dancing are a credit to the seminary. Her manners—which have caused you to call her Princess Sara—are perfect. Her friendliness she exhibits by giving you this afternoon's party. I hope you appreciate her generosity. I wish you to express your appreciation of it by saying aloud all together, 'Thank you, Sara!'"

The entire schoolroom rose to its feet and did so.

Sara made a shy curtsy—a very nice one. "Thank you," she said, "for coming to my party."

"Very pretty, indeed, Sara. That is what a real princess does when the populace applauds her."

Then Miss Minchin added, "Lavinia, the sound you just made was extremely like a snort. If you are jealous, I beg you will express your feelings in a more ladylike manner. Now I will leave you to enjoy yourselves."

The instant she swept out of the room, her spell was broken and every seat was empty. There was a rush toward the boxes. Sara bent over one of them with a delighted face.

"These are books, I know," she said.

The little children broke into a rueful murmur, and Ermengarde looked aghast.

"Does your papa send you books for a birthday present?" she exclaimed. "Why, he's as bad as mine. Don't open them, Sara."

"I like them," Sara laughed, but she turned to the biggest box. When she took out the Last Doll it was so magnificent that the children uttered groans of joy and drew back to gaze at it in breathless wonder.

"She is almost as big as Lottie," someone gasped.

Lottie clapped her hands and danced about, giggling.

"She's dressed for the theater," said Lavinia. "Her cloak is lined with ermine."

"Oh," cried Ermengarde, darting forward, "she has an opera-glass in her hand—a blue-and-gold one!"

"Here is her trunk," said Sara. "Let us open it and look at her things."

She sat on the floor and turned the key. The children crowded around her as she lifted tray after tray and revealed their contents. Never had the schoolroom been in such an uproar. There were lace collars and silk stockings and handkerchiefs; there was a jewel case containing a necklace and a tiara which looked as if they were made of real diamonds; there was a long sealskin and muff; there were ball dresses and walking dresses and visiting dresses; there were hats and tea gowns and fans. Even Lavinia and Jessie forgot they were too elderly to care for dolls.

"Suppose," Sara said, "suppose she understands human talk and feels proud of being admired."

"You are always supposing things," said Lavinia, and her air was very superior.

"I know I am," answered Sara, undisturbed. "I like it."

"It's all very well to suppose things if you have everything," said Lavinia. "Could you suppose and pretend if you were a beggar and lived in a garret?"

Sara stopped arranging the Last Doll's ostrich plumes and looked thoughtful.

"I believe I could," she said. "If one was a beggar, one would have to suppose and pretend all the time. But it might not be easy."

She often thought afterward how strange it was that just as she had finished saying this—just at that very moment—Miss Amelia came into the room.

"Sara," she said, "your papa's attorney, Mr. Barrow, has called to see Miss Minchin. As she must talk to him alone and the refreshments are set out in her parlor, you had all better come and have your feast now so that she can speak with him here in the schoolroom."

Refreshments were not disdained at any hour, and many pairs of eyes gleamed. They all left the Last Doll sitting upon a chair with the glories of her wardrobe scattered about her— dresses and coats and piles of lace-frilled petticoats.

Becky, who was not offered any refreshments, lingered a moment to look at these beauties. She picked up first a muff and then a coat, and while she stood looking at them, she heard Miss Minchin coming. In terror of a scolding, she darted under the corner table.

Miss Minchin came into the room, accompanied by a sharp-featured, dry little lawyer. She gazed at him with an irritated and puzzled expression, sat down with stiff dignity, and waved him to a chair.

"Pray, be seated, Mr. Barrow."

Mr. Barrow did not sit down. He put on his eyeglasses and looked at the Last Doll and the things which surrounded her. The Last Doll herself did not seem to mind; she merely sat upright and returned his gaze.

"A hundred pounds," he remarked. "Expensive material, the work of a Parisian fashion designer. He spent money lavishly, that young man."

"I beg your pardon, Mr. Barrow," she said stiffly.

"Birthday presents to a child eleven years old! Mad extravagance, I call it."

Miss Minchin drew herself up still more rigidly.

"Captain Crewe is a man of fortune," she said. "The diamond mines alone—"

Mr. Barrow wheeled round upon her. "Diamond mines!" he broke out. "There are none! Never were!"

Miss Minchin got up. "What!" she cried. "What do you mean?"

"At any rate," answered Mr. Barrow, snappishly, "it would have been much better if there never had been any. Diamond mines or gold mines or any other kind of mines spell ruin more often than they spell wealth, when a man puts his money into the hands of a dear friend and is not a businessman himself. The late Captain Crewe—"

Here Miss Minchin stopped him with a gasp.

"The *late* Captain Crewe?" she cried out. "The *late?* You don't come to tell me that Captain Crewe is—?"

"He's dead, ma'am," Mr. Barrow answered. "Died of jungle fever and business troubles combined. The jungle fever might not have killed him if he had not been driven mad by the business troubles, and the business troubles might not have put an end to him if the jungle fever had not assisted. Captain Crewe is dead!"

Miss Minchin dropped into her chair again.

"What business troubles?"

"Diamond mines, and dear friends—and ruin."

"Ruin!" she gasped out.

"Lost every penny. The dear friend put all his own money into it, and all Captain Crewe's. Then the dear friend ran away. Captain Crewe had a fever when the news came. The shock was too much for him. He died delirious, raving about his little girl—and didn't leave a penny."

Miss Minchin had never received such a blow in her life.

"Do you mean to tell me," she cried out, "that he left nothing? That Sara will have no fortune? That she is left on my hands a little pauper instead of an heiress?"

"She is certainly left a beggar," he replied. "And she is certainly left on your hands, ma'am—as she hasn't a relation in the world that we know of."

"It is monstrous!" she said. "She's in my sitting room at this moment, dressed in silk gauze and lace petticoats, giving a party at my expense."

"She's giving it at your expense, madam, if she's giving it," Mr. Barrow agreed calmly. "Barrow and Skipworth are not responsible for anything. There never was a cleaner sweep made of a man's fortune. Captain Crewe died without paying our last bill—and it was a big one."

"That is what has happened to me!" she cried. "I was always so sure of his payments that I went to all sorts of ridiculous expenses for the child. I paid the bills for that ridiculous doll and her ridiculous wardrobe. She has a carriage and a pony and a maid, and I've paid for all of them since the last check came."

Mr. Barrow did not feel any sympathy for irate keepers of boarding schools.

"You had better not pay for anything more, ma'am," he remarked, "unless you want to make presents to the young lady. She hasn't a brass farthing to call her own."

"But what am I to do?" demanded Miss Minchin.

"There isn't anything to do," said Mr. Barrow, folding up his eyeglasses and slipping them into his pocket. "Captain Crewe is dead. The child is a pauper. Nobody is responsible for her but you."

"I am not responsible for her, and I refuse to be made responsible!" Miss Minchin was white with rage. "If you think she is to be foisted off on me, you are greatly mistaken. I have been robbed and cheated. I will turn her out into the street!"

Mr. Barrow moved toward the door. "I wouldn't do that, madam; it wouldn't look good. Unpleasant story to get about." He was a clever businessman, and he knew that Miss Minchin was a shrewd businesswoman who would see the truth. She could not afford to do a thing that would make people speak of her as cruel and hard-hearted.

"Better keep her and make use of her. She's a clever child, I do believe. You can get a good deal out of her as she grows older."

"I will get a good deal out of her before she grows older!"

"I am sure you will, ma'am," said Mr. Barrow, with a little sinister smile. "I am sure you will."

He bowed himself out and closed the door, and Miss Minchin stood for a few moments and glared at it. Her star pupil had melted into nothingness, leaving only a friendless little beggar girl. The money she had advanced could not be regained.

As she stood there breathless, she heard a burst of gay voices from the feast in her own sacred room. As she started toward the door, it was opened by Miss Amelia, who fell back a step in alarm at the sight of her face.

"What *is* the matter, Sister?"

"Where is Sara Crewe? Has she a black frock in her sumptuous wardrobe?"

"Sara? A black frock?" Miss Amelia stammered. "A *black* one?"

"She has frocks of every other color. Has she a black one?"

Miss Amelia began to turn pale. "No—ye-es!" she said. "But it is too short for her. She has only the old black velvet, and she has outgrown it."

"Go and tell her to take off that preposterous pink silk gauze, and put the black one on, whether it is too short or not. She is through with finery!"

Miss Amelia began to wring her fat hands and cried, "What has happened?"

"Captain Crewe is dead," Miss Minchin said. "He has died without a penny. That spoiled child is left a pauper on my hands."

Miss Amelia sat down heavily in the nearest chair.

"Hundreds of pounds have I spent on nonsense for her. And I shall never see a penny of it. Put a stop to this ridiculous party of hers. Go and make her change her frock at once."

"I?" panted Miss Amelia. "M—must I go and tell her now?"

"This moment!" was the fierce answer. "Don't sit staring like a goose. Go!"

Poor Miss Amelia was accustomed to being called a goose. She knew that she was rather a goose, and that it was left to geese to do a great many disagreeable things. When her older sister looked and spoke fiercely as she had done just now, the wisest course was to obey orders without any comment.

During the last year the story of the diamond mines had suggested all sorts of possibilities to Miss Minchin. Even owners of girls' schools might make fortunes in stock investments, with the aid of owners of mines. But now that hope was gone.

"Princess Sara, indeed!" she said. "The child has been pampered as if she were a queen."

She was sweeping angrily past the corner table as she said it, and she heard a loud, sobbing sniff.

"What is that?" The loud, sobbing sniff was heard again, and she stooped and raised the hanging folds of the tablecloth.

"How dare you!" she cried out. "How dare you! Come out immediately!"

It was poor Becky who crawled out. Her cap was knocked on one side, and her face was red with repressed crying.

"If you please, 'm—it's me, mum," she explained. "I was lookin' at the doll, mum, an' I was frightened when you come in—an' slipped under the table."

"You have been there all the time, listening," said Miss Minchin.

"No, mum," Becky protested, bobbing curtsies. "Not listenin'. I wouldn't listen for nothin'. But I couldn't help hearin'." Suddenly it seemed as if she lost all fear of the awful lady before her. She burst into fresh tears.

"Leave the room!" ordered Miss Minchin.

Becky curtsied again, the tears openly streaming down her cheeks.

"Yes, 'm; I will, 'm," she said, trembling. "But oh, Miss Sara's been such a rich young lady, an' she's been waited on, 'and and foot; an' what will she do now, mum, without no maid? If—if, oh please, would you let me wait on her after I've done my pots an' kettles? Oh," breaking out afresh, "poor little Miss Sara, mum—that was called a princess."

Somehow this made Miss Minchin feel more angry than ever.

"No—certainly not," she said. "She will wait on herself, and on other people, too. Leave the room this instant."

Becky threw her apron over her head and fled. She ran out of the room and down the steps into the scullery, and there she sat down among her pots and kettles and wept as if her heart would break.

"It's exactly like the ones in the stories," she wailed. "Them pore princess ones that was drove into the world."

* * *

Miss Minchin had never looked so still and hard as she did when Sara came to her a few hours later. Even by that time it seemed to Sara as if the birthday party had either been a dream or had happened years ago, and had happened in the life of another little girl.

Every sign of the festivities had been swept away; the holly had been removed from the schoolroom walls, and the desks were back in their places. Miss Minchin's sitting room looked as it always did—all traces of the feast were gone, and she was wearing her usual dress. The pupils had been ordered to put away their party frocks. This having been done, they had returned to the schoolroom and huddled together in groups, whispering and talking.

"Tell Sara to come to my room," Miss Minchin said to her sister. "And tell her I will have no crying or unpleasant scenes."

"Sister," replied Miss Amelia, "she is the strangest child I ever saw. She has made no fuss at all. You remember she made none when Captain Crewe went back to India. When I told her what had happened, she just stood still and looked at me without making a sound. Her eyes got bigger and bigger, and she went quite pale. When I had finished, she still stood staring for a few seconds, and then her chin began to shake, and she turned round and ran out of the room and upstairs. Several of the other children began to cry, but she did not seem to hear them or to be alive to anything but just what I was saying. It made me feel queer not to be answered; you expect people will say *something*—whatever it is."

Nobody but Sara ever knew what happened in her room after she had run upstairs and locked her door. She herself scarcely remembered anything but that she walked up and down, saying over and over again to herself in a voice that did not seem her own, "My papa is dead! My papa is dead!"

Once she stopped before Emily, who sat watching her from her chair, and cried out, "Emily! Do you hear? Do you hear Papa is dead? He is dead in India—thousands of miles away."

When she came into Miss Minchin's sitting room in answer to her summons, her face was white and her eyes had dark rings around them. Her mouth was set as if she did not wish it to reveal what she was suffering. She did not look in the least like the rose-colored butterfly child who had flown about from one of her treasures to the other in the decorated schoolroom. She was a strange, desolate, almost grotesque little figure.

Without Mariette's help, she had put on the old black-velvet frock. It was too short and tight, and in her dark stockings her slender legs looked long and thin. As she had not found a piece of black ribbon, her short, thick black hair tumbled loosely about her white face. She held Emily tightly in one arm, draped in a piece of black cloth.

"Put down your doll," said Miss Minchin. "What do you mean by bringing her here?"

"No," Sara answered. "I will not put her down. She is all I have. My papa gave her to me."

She had always made Miss Minchin feel secretly uncomfortable, and she did so now—perhaps because Miss Minchin knew she was doing a heartless and inhuman thing.

"You will have no time for dolls in future," she said. "You will have to work and make yourself useful."

Sara kept her big, strange eyes fixed on her, and said not a word.

"Everything will be very different now," Miss Minchin went on. "I suppose Miss Amelia has explained matters to you.

"Yes," answered Sara. "My papa is dead. He left me no money. I am quite poor."

"You are a beggar," said Miss Minchin, her temper rising at the recollection of what this meant to herself. "It appears that you have no relations and no home, and no one to take care of you."

For a moment the thin, pale little face twitched, but Sara again said nothing.

"What are you staring at?" demanded Miss Minchin. "Are you so stupid that you cannot understand? I tell you that you are quite alone in the world and have no one to do anything for you unless I choose to keep you here out of charity."

"I understand," answered Sara, in a low tone, and there was a sound as if she had gulped down something which rose in her throat. "I understand."

"That doll," cried Miss Minchin, pointing to the splendid birthday gift seated nearby—"that ridiculous doll, with all her nonsensical, extravagant things—I actually paid the bill for her!"

Sara turned her head toward the chair.

"The Last Doll," she said. "The Last Doll." And her little mournful voice had an odd sound.

"The Last Doll, indeed!" said Miss Minchin. "And she is mine, not yours. Everything you own is mine."

"Please take it away from me, then," said Sara. "I do not want it."

72

If she had cried and sobbed and seemed frightened, Miss Minchin might almost have had more patience with her. She was a woman who liked to domineer and feel her power, and as she looked at Sara's pale little steadfast face and heard her proud little voice, she felt powerless.

"Don't put on grand airs," she said. "The time for that sort of thing is past. You are not a princess any longer. Your carriage and your pony will be sent away—your maid will be dismissed. You will wear your oldest and plainest clothes—your extravagant ones are no longer suited to your station. You are like Becky—you must work for your living."

To her surprise, a faint gleam of light came into the child's eyes—a shade of relief.

"Can I work?" she said. "If I can work it will not matter so much. What can I do?"

"You can do anything you are told," was the answer. "You are a sharp child and pick up things readily. If you make yourself useful I may let you stay here. You speak French well, and you can help with the younger children."

"May I?" exclaimed Sara. "Oh, please let me! I know I can teach them. I like them, and they like me."

"Don't talk nonsense about people liking you," said Miss Minchin. "You will have to do more than teach the little ones. You will run errands and help in the kitchen as well as in the schoolroom. If you don't please me, you will be sent away. Remember that. Now go."

Sara stood still just a moment, looking at her. In her young soul, she was thinking deep and strange things. Then she turned to leave the room.

"Stop!" said Miss Minchin. "Don't you intend to thank me?"

Sara paused, and all the deep, strange thoughts surged up in her breast.

"What for?" she said.

"For my kindness to you," replied Miss Minchin. "For my kindness in giving you a home."

Sara made two or three steps toward her. Her thin little chest heaved up and down, and she spoke in a strange unchildish way.

"You are not kind," she said. "You are not kind, and it is not a home." And she turned and ran out of the room before Miss Minchin could do anything but stare after her with stony anger.

She went up the stairs slowly, but panting for breath, and she held Emily tightly against her side.

"I wish she could talk," she said to herself. "If only she could speak!"

She meant to go to her room and lie down on the tiger skin with her cheek upon the great cat's head, and look into the fire and think and think and think. But just before she reached the landing Miss Amelia came out of the door and closed it behind her, and stood before it looking nervous and awkward. The truth was that she felt ashamed of the thing she had been ordered to do.

"You—you are not to go in there," she said.

"Not go in?" exclaimed Sara, and she fell back a pace.

"That is not your room now," Miss Amelia answered, reddening a little.

All at once Sara understood. She realized that this was the beginning of the change Miss Minchin had spoken of.

"Where is my room?" she asked, hoping very much that her voice did not shake.

"You are to sleep in the attic room next to Becky's."

Sara knew where it was. Becky had told her about it. She turned and mounted up two flights of stairs. The last one was narrow and covered with shabby strips of old carpet. She felt as if she were walking away and leaving far behind her the world in which that other child, who no longer seemed herself, had lived. This child, in her short, tight old frock, climbing the stairs to the attic, was quite a different creature.

When she reached the attic door and opened it, her heart gave a dreary little thump. Then she shut the door and stood against it and looked about her.

Yes, this was another world. The room had a slanting roof and was whitewashed. The whitewash was dingy and had fallen off in places. There was a rusty grate, an old iron bedstead, and a hard bed covered with a faded coverlet. Some pieces of furniture too much worn to be used downstairs had been sent up. Under the skylight in the roof, which showed nothing but an oblong piece of dull gray sky, there stood an old battered red footstool. Sara went to it and sat down. She seldom cried. She did not cry now. She laid Emily across her knees and put her face down upon her and her arms around her, and sat there, her little black head resting on the black cloth, not saying one word, not making one sound.

And as she sat in this silence there came a low tap at the door—such a low, humble one that she did not at first hear it and was not roused until the door was timidly pushed open and a poor, tear-smeared face appeared peeping round it. It was Becky's face. She had been crying for hours and rubbing her eyes with her kitchen apron until she looked strange indeed.

"Oh, miss," she said under her breath. "Might I—would you allow me—jest to come in?"

Sara lifted her head and looked at her. She tried to begin a smile, and somehow she could not. Suddenly—because of the loving mournfulness of Becky's streaming eyes—her face looked more like a child's not too old for her years. She held out her hand and gave a little sob.

"Oh, Becky," she said. "I told you we were just the same—only two little girls—just two little girls. You see how true it is. There's no difference now. I'm not a princess anymore."

Becky ran to her and caught her hand, kneeling beside her and sobbing with love and pain.

"Yes, miss, you are," she cried, and her words were all broken. "Whats'ever 'appens to you—whats'ever—you'd be a princess all the same—an' nothin' couldn't make you nothin' different."

8
IN THE ATTIC

SARA NEVER FORGOT the first night she spent in her attic. All night, she lived through a wild, unchildlike woe of which she never spoke to anyone. There was no one who would have understood. "My papa is dead!" she kept whispering to herself. "My papa is dead!"

It was not until long afterward that she realized that her bed had been so hard that she turned over and over in it to find a place to rest, that the darkness seemed more intense than any she had ever known, and that the wind howled over the roof among the chimneys like something in pain. Then there was something worse—scufflings and scratchings and squeakings in the walls. She knew what they meant, because Becky had described them. They meant rats and mice who were either fighting or playing together. Once or twice she even heard sharp-toed feet scurrying across the floor, and when first she heard them she sat up in bed trembling, then lay down and covered her head with the bedclothes.

The change in her life did not come about gradually but all at once.

"She must begin as she is to go on," Miss Minchin said to Miss Amelia. "She must be taught at once what she is to expect."

Mariette had left the house the next morning. The glimpse Sara caught of her own sitting room, as she passed its open door, showed her that everything had been changed. Her ornaments and luxuries had been removed, and a bed had been placed in a corner to transform it into a new pupil's bedroom.

When she went down to breakfast she saw that her seat at Miss Minchin's side was occupied by Lavinia.

"You will begin your new duties, Sara," Miss Minchin said coldly, "by taking your seat with the younger children at a smaller table. You must keep them quiet and see that they behave well and do not waste their food. You ought to have been down earlier. Lottie has already spilled her tea."

That was the beginning, and from day to day her duties increased. She taught the younger children French and heard their other lessons. It was found that she could be made use of in numberless directions. She could be sent on errands at any time and in all weathers. She could be told to do things other people neglected. The cook and the housemaids enjoyed ordering her about. They were not the best servants, with neither good manners nor good tempers, and it was frequently convenient for them to have someone to blame.

During the first month or two, Sara thought that her willingness to do things as well as she could might soften those who drove her so hard. In her proud little heart she wanted them to see that she was trying to earn her living and not accepting charity. But the time came when she saw that no one was softened at all. The more willing she was to do as she was told, the more domineering the careless housemaids became, and the quicker the cook was to scold and blame her.

If Sara had been older, Miss Minchin would have given her the bigger girls to teach and saved money by dismissing an adult teacher. But since she was still a child, she was more useful as a little errand girl and maid of all work. An ordinary errand boy would not have been so clever and reliable. Sara could be trusted with difficult assignments and complicated messages. She could even go and pay bills, and she combined with this the ability to dust a room well and to set things in order.

Her own lessons became things of the past. She was taught nothing, and only after long and busy days spent in running here and there at everybody's orders was she grudgingly allowed to go into the deserted schoolroom with a pile of old books and study alone at night.

"If I do not remind myself of the things I have learned, perhaps I may forget them," she said to herself. "I am almost a scullery maid, and if I am a scullery maid who knows nothing, I shall be like poor Becky. I wonder if I could begin to drop my *h*s and not remember that Henry the Eighth had six wives."

One of the most curious things in her new existence was her changed position among the pupils. Instead of being a royal personage among them, she no longer seemed one of their number at all. She was kept so constantly at work that she scarcely ever had an opportunity of speaking to any of them, and it was clear that Miss Minchin preferred it that way.

"I will not have her talking to the other children," that lady said. "Girls like a grievance, and if she begins to tell romantic stories about herself, she will seem like a victim, and parents will be given a wrong impression. It is better that she should live a separate life—one suited to her circumstances. I am giving her a home, and that is more than she has any right to expect from me."

Sara did not expect much and was far too proud to try to fit in with girls who felt awkward and uncertain about her. In fact,

Miss Minchin's pupils were dull, matter-of-fact girls. They were used to being rich and comfortable, and as Sara's frocks grew shorter and shabbier and queerer-looking, and it became known that she wore shoes with holes in them and was sent out to buy groceries and carry them through the streets in a basket, they didn't know how to speak to her.

"To think that she was the girl with the diamond mines," Lavinia commented. "She does look a sight. And she's queerer than ever. I never liked her much, but I can't bear that way she has now of looking at people without speaking—just as if she was figuring them out."

"I am," said Sara to herself when she heard of this. "That's what I look at some people for. I like to know about them. I think them over afterward."

The truth was that she had saved herself trouble several times by keeping her eye on Lavinia, who was quite ready to make mischief.

Sara never interfered with anyone. She worked like a drudge; she tramped through the wet streets, carrying parcels and baskets; she labored with the little childrens' French lessons; as she became shabbier and more forlorn-looking, she was told that she had better take her meals downstairs; she was treated as if she was nobody's concern, and her heart grew proud and sore, but she never told anyone what she felt.

"Soldiers don't complain," she would say to herself. "I will pretend this is part of a war."

There were hours when her heart might almost have broken with loneliness but for three people.

The first was Becky. Throughout all that first night in the garret, she had felt a vague comfort in knowing that on the other side of the wall in which the rats scuffled and squeaked there was another young human creature. And during the nights that followed, the sense of comfort grew. They had little chance to speak to each other during the day. Each had her own tasks to perform, and any attempt at conversation would have been regarded as loitering.

Before daybreak Becky used to slip into Sara's attic and button her dress and give her such help as she required before she went downstairs to light the kitchen fire. And when night came Sara always heard the humble knock at her door which meant that her handmaid was ready to help her again if she was needed. During the first weeks of her grief, Sara felt as if she were too numb to talk, and Becky's heart told her that it was best that people in trouble should be left alone.

The second of the trio of comforters was Ermengarde, but odd things happened before Ermengarde found her place.

When Sara's mind awakened again to the life about her, she realized that she had forgotten all about Ermengarde. The two had always been friends, but Ermengarde was as dull as she was affectionate. She had clung to Sara in a simple, helpless way; she had brought her lessons to her for help; she had listened to her every word and besieged her with requests for stories. But she had nothing interesting to say herself, and she loathed books of every description. She was not a person one would remember when one was caught in the storm of a great trouble.

It had been all the easier to forget her because she had been suddenly called home for a few weeks. When she came back she did not see Sara for a day or two, and she finally encountered her carrying lots of pupils' clothes downstairs to be mended. (Sara herself had already been taught to mend them.) Sara looked pale and unlike herself.

Ermengarde was too slow a girl for such a situation. She could not think of anything to say. She knew what had happened, but she had never imagined Sara could look like this—so odd and poor and like a servant. It made her miserable, and she could do nothing but break into a short hysterical laugh and exclaim aimlessly, "Oh, Sara, is that you?"

"Yes," answered Sara, and her face flushed.

She held the pile of garments in her arms, and her chin rested upon the top of it to keep it steady. Something in the look of her straight-gazing eyes made Ermengarde lose her wits still more. She felt as if Sara had changed into a new kind of girl, and she had never known her before.

"Oh," she stammered. "How—how are you?"

"I don't know," Sara replied. "How are you?"

"I'm—I'm quite well," said Ermengarde, overwhelmed with shyness. Then she thought of something to say. "Are you—are you very unhappy?"

Then Sara was guilty of an injustice. Just at that moment her torn heart swelled within her, and she felt that if anyone was as stupid as that, one had better get away from her.

"What do you think?" she said. "Do you think I am very happy?" And she marched past her without another word.

She later realized that if her wretchedness had not made her forget things, she would have known that poor, dull Ermengarde was not to be blamed for her awkward ways. She was always awkward, and the more she felt, the more stupid she acted.

"She is like the others," Sara had thought mistakenly. "She does not really want to talk to me. No one does."

So for several weeks a barrier stood between them. When they met by chance Sara looked the other way, and Ermengarde felt too embarrassed to speak. Sometimes they nodded to each other in passing, but there were times when they did not even say hello.

She had never imagined Sara could look like this—
so odd and poor and like a servant.

"If she would rather not talk to me," Sara thought, "I will keep out of her way. Miss Minchin makes that easy enough."

Miss Minchin made it so easy that they scarcely saw each other at all. Ermengarde grew more dull than ever, and she looked listless and unhappy. She used to sit in the window seat, huddled in a heap, and stare out of the window without speaking. Once Jessie, who was passing, stopped to look at her curiously.

"What are you crying for, Ermengarde?" she asked.

"I'm not crying," answered Ermengarde, in a muffled, unsteady voice.

"You are," said Jessie. "A great big tear just rolled down the bridge of your nose and dropped off at the end of it. And there goes another."

"Well," said Ermengarde, "I'm miserable—and no one need interfere." And she turned her plump back and took out her handkerchief and hid her face in it.

That night Sara went to her attic later than usual. She had been kept at work until after the time the pupils went to bed, and after that she had gone to her lessons in the lonely schoolroom. When she reached the top of the stairs, she was surprised to see a glimmer of light coming from under the attic door.

"Nobody goes there but myself," she thought quickly, "but someone has lighted a candle."

Someone had, indeed, lighted a candle. The someone was sitting upon the battered footstool and was dressed in her nightgown and wrapped up in a red shawl. It was Ermengarde.

"Ermengarde!" cried Sara. She was so startled that she was almost frightened. "You will get into trouble."

Ermengarde stumbled up from her footstool. She shuffled across the attic in her bedroom slippers, which were too large for her. Her eyes and nose were pink from crying.

"I know I shall—if I'm found out," she said. "But I don't care—I don't care a bit. Oh, Sara, please tell me. What is the matter? Why don't you like me any more?"

Something in her voice made the familiar lump rise in Sara's throat. It was so affectionate and simple—so like the old Ermengarde who had asked to be best friends.

"I do like you," Sara answered. "I thought—you see, everything is different now. I thought you—were different."

Ermengarde opened her wet eyes wide. "Why, it was you who were different!" she cried. "You didn't want to talk to me. I didn't know what to do. It was you who were different after I came back."

Sara thought a moment. She saw she had made a mistake.

"I *am* different," she explained, "though not in the way you think. Miss Minchin does not want me to talk to the girls. Most of them don't want to talk to me. I thought—perhaps—you didn't. So I tried to keep out of your way."

"Oh, Sara," Ermengarde almost wailed. And then after one more look they rushed into each other's arms. Sara's small black head lay for some minutes on the shoulder covered by the red shawl.

Afterward they sat on the floor together, Sara clasping her knees with her arms, and Ermengarde rolled up in her shawl. Ermengarde looked at the odd, big-eyed little face adoringly.

"I couldn't bear it any more," she said. "I dare say you could live without me, Sara, but I couldn't live without you. I was nearly dead. So tonight when I was crying under the bed-clothes, I thought all at once of creeping up here and just begging you to let us be friends again."

"You are nicer than I am," said Sara. "I was too proud to try and make friends. You see, now that trials have come, they have shown that I am not a nice girl. Perhaps"—wrinkling her forehead wisely—"that is what they were sent for."

"I don't see any good in them," said Ermengarde stoutly.

"Neither do I—to speak the truth," admitted Sara, frankly. "But I suppose there *might* be good in things, even if we don't see it. There *might*"—doubtfully—"be good in Miss Minchin."

Ermengarde looked round the attic with timid curiosity.

"Sara," she said, "do you think you can bear living here?"

Sara looked round also.

"If I pretend it's quite different, I can," she answered. "Or if I pretend it is a place in a story."

She spoke slowly. Her imagination was beginning to work. It had not been working for her at all since her troubles had come upon her.

"Other people have lived in worse places. Think of the Count of Monte Cristo in the dungeon. And think of the people in the Bastille!"

"The Bastille," half whispered Ermengarde, watching her and beginning to be fascinated. She remembered stories of the French Revolution which Sara had been able to fix in her mind by her dramatic descriptions. No one but Sara could have done it.

A well-known glow came into Sara's eyes.

"Yes," she said, hugging her knees, "that will be a good place to pretend about. I am a prisoner in the Bastille. I have been here for years and years and years. Everybody has forgotten about me. Miss Minchin is the jailer, and Becky"—a sudden light adding itself to the glow in her eyes—"Becky is the prisoner in the next cell."

She turned to Ermengarde, looking like the old Sara.

"I shall pretend that," she said, "and it will be a great comfort."

Ermengarde was at once enraptured.

"And will you tell me all about it?" she said. "May I creep up here at night, whenever it is safe, and hear the things you have made up in the day? It will seem as if we were more best friends than ever."

"Yes," answered Sara, nodding. "Adversity tests people, and mine has tested you and proved how nice you are."

9

MELCHISEDEC

THE THIRD PERSON in the trio was Lottie. She was a small thing and she could not understand why Sara looked different—why she wore an old black frock and came into the schoolroom only to teach instead of to sit in her place of honor and learn lessons herself. Lottie's chief difficulty was that Sara said so little when one asked her questions. At seven, mysteries must be made clear if one is to understand them.

"Are you very poor now, Sara?" she had asked the first morning her friend took charge of the small French class. "Are you as poor as a beggar?" She thrust a fat hand into the slim one and opened round, tearful eyes. "I don't want you to be as poor as a beggar."

She looked as if she was going to cry. And Sara hurriedly consoled her.

"Beggars have nowhere to live," she said courageously. "I have a place to live."

"Where do you live?" persisted Lottie. "The new girl sleeps in your room, and it isn't pretty anymore."

"I live in another room," said Sara.

"Is it a nice one?" inquired Lottie. "I want to go and see it."

"You must not talk," said Sara. "Miss Minchin is looking at us.

She will be angry with me for letting you whisper."

She had found out already that she was to be held accountable for everything. If the children were not attentive, if they talked, if they were restless, she would be blamed.

But Lottie was a determined little person. If Sara would not tell her where she lived, she would find out in some other way. She hung about the older girls and listened, and acting upon certain information they had let drop, she started late one afternoon on a voyage of discovery, climbing stairs she had never known the existence of, until she reached the attic floor. There she found two doors near each other, and opening one, she saw her beloved Sara standing upon an old table and looking out an open window.

"Sara!" she cried, aghast. "Mamma Sara!" She was aghast because the attic was so bare and ugly and seemed so far away from all the world.

Sara turned round at the sound of her voice. It was her turn to be aghast. She jumped down from her table and ran to the child.

"Don't cry and make a noise," she implored. "I shall be scolded if you do, and I have been scolded all day. It's—it's not such a bad room, Lottie."

"Isn't it?" gasped Lottie. She was a spoiled child, but she was fond enough of her adopted parent to make an effort to keep quiet for her sake. Perhaps any place in which Sara lived might turn out to be nice. "Why isn't it bad, Sara?" she almost whispered.

Sara hugged her close and tried to laugh. There was a comfort in the warmth of the plump, childish body. Sara had had a hard day and had been staring out the window with hot eyes.

"You can see all sorts of things you can't see downstairs," she said.

"What sort of things?" demanded Lottie, with that curiosity Sara could always awaken even in bigger girls.

"Chimneys—quite close to us—with smoke curling up in wreaths and clouds and going up into the sky. And sparrows hopping about and talking to each other just as if they were people. And other attic windows where heads may pop out any minute and you can wonder who they belong to. And it all feels as high up—as if it was another world."

"Oh, let me see it!" cried Lottie. "Lift me up!"

Sara lifted her up, and they stood on the old table together and leaned on the edge of the window in the roof and looked out.

Anyone who has not done this does not know what a different world they saw. The roof slates spread out on either side of them and slanted down into the rain gutter-pipes. The sparrows, being at home there, twittered and hopped about without fear. Two of them perched on the chimney top nearest and quarreled with each other until one pecked the other and drove him away. The garret window next to theirs was shut because the house next door was empty.

"I wish someone lived there," Sara said. "It is so close, sharing the same roof, that if there was a little girl in that attic we could talk to each other through the windows and climb over to see each other if we were not afraid of falling."

The sky seemed so much nearer than when one saw it from the street that Lottie was enchanted. From the attic window among the chimney pots, the things which were happening in the world below seemed almost unreal. One scarcely believed in the existence of Miss Minchin and Miss Amelia and the schoolroom, and the roll of wheels in the square seemed a sound belonging to another existence.

"Oh, Sara!" cried Lottie, "I like this attic—I like it! It is nicer than downstairs!"

90

"Look at that sparrow," whispered Sara. "I wish I had some crumbs to throw to him."

"I have some!" came in a little shriek from Lottie. "I have part of a bun in my pocket. I bought it with my penny yesterday, and I saved a bit."

When they threw out a few crumbs the sparrow jumped and flew away to an adjacent chimney top. The unexpected crumbs startled him. But when Lottie remained still and Sara chirped softly—almost as if she were a sparrow herself—he put his head to one side, and from his perch on the chimney looked down at the crumbs with twinkling eyes. Lottie could scarcely keep still.

"Will he come? Will he come?" she whispered.

"His eyes look as if he would," Sara whispered back. "He is thinking and thinking whether he dare. Yes, he will! Yes, he is coming!"

He flew down and hopped toward the crumbs, but stopped a few inches away from them, putting his head to one side again, as if reflecting on the chance that Sara and Lottie might turn out to be big cats and jump on him. At last his heart told him they were nicer than they looked, and he hopped nearer and nearer, darted at the biggest crumb with a lightning peck, seized it, and carried it away to the other side of his chimney.

"Now he knows," said Sara. "And he will come back for the others."

He did come back and even brought a friend, and the friend went away and brought a relative, and among them they made a hearty meal over which they twittered and chattered and exclaimed, stopping every now and then to put their heads to one side and examine Lottie and Sara. Lottie was so delighted that she forgot her first shocked impression of the attic. In fact, when she was lifted down from the table Sara was able to point out to her many beauties in the room which she herself had not suspected.

"It is so little and so high above everything," she said, "that it is almost like a nest in a tree. The slanting ceiling is so funny. See, you can scarcely stand up at this end of the room. And when the morning begins to come I can lie in bed and look right up into the sky through that flat window in the roof. It is like a square patch of light. If the sun is going to shine, little pink clouds float about, and I feel as if I could touch them. And if it rains, the drops patter and patter as if they were saying something nice. Then if there are stars, you can lie and try to count how many go into the patch. And just look at that tiny, rusty grate in the corner. If it was polished and there was a fire in it, just think how nice it would be. You see, it's really a beautiful little room."

She was walking round the small place, holding Lottie's hand and making gestures that described all the beauties she was making herself see. She made Lottie see them, too.

"You see," she said, "there could be a thick, soft blue Indian rug on the floor; and in that corner there could be a soft little sofa, with cushions to curl up on; and just over it could be a shelf full of books so that one could reach them easily; and there could be a fur rug before the fire, and hangings on the wall to cover up the whitewash, and pictures. They would have to be little ones, but they could be beautiful. And there could be a lamp with a deep rose-colored shade; and a table in the middle with things to have tea with; and a little fat copper kettle singing on the hob; and the bed could be quite different. It could be made soft and covered with a lovely silk coverlet. And perhaps we could coax the sparrows until we made such friends with them that they would come and peck at the window and ask to be let in."

"Oh, Sara!" cried Lottie. "I should like to live here!"

When Sara had persuaded her to go downstairs again, she stood in the middle of the room and looked about. The enchantment of her imaginings had died away. The bed was hard and covered with its dingy quilt. The whitewashed wall showed its broken patches, the floor was cold and bare, the grate was broken and rusty, and the battered footstool was the only seat in the room. She sat down on it for a few minutes and let her head drop in her hands. That Lottie had come and gone away again made things seem a little worse—just as perhaps prisoners feel a little more desolate after visitors come and go, leaving them behind.

"It's a lonely place," she said. "Sometimes it's the loneliest place in the world."

She was sitting in this way when her attention was attracted by a slight sound near her. A large rat was sitting up on his hind quarters and sniffing the air in an interested manner. Some of Lottie's crumbs had dropped upon the floor and their scent had drawn him out of his hole.

He looked so queer and so like a gray-whiskered dwarf or gnome that Sara was fascinated. He looked at her with his bright eyes, as if he were asking a question.

"I dare say it is rather hard to be a rat," she mused. "Nobody likes you. People jump and run away and scream out, 'Oh, a horrid rat!' But nobody asked this rat if he wanted to be a rat when he was made. Nobody said, 'Wouldn't you rather be a sparrow?'"

She sat so quietly that the rat began to take courage. He was much afraid of her, but perhaps he had a heart like the sparrow and it told him that she was not a thing which pounced. He was very hungry.

"Come on," said Sara, "I'm not a trap. You can have them,

poor thing! Prisoners in the Bastille used to make friends with rats. Suppose I make friends with you."

How animals understand things I do not know, but it is certain that they do understand. Perhaps there is a language not made of words, and everything in the world understands it. Whatever the reason, the rat knew from that moment that he was safe. He knew that this young human being sitting on the red footstool would not jump up and throw heavy objects at him that would send him limping back to his hole. He was really a very nice rat, and did not mean the least harm. When he had stood on his hind legs and sniffed the air with his bright eyes fixed on Sara, he had hoped that she would understand this. He went softly toward the crumbs and began to eat them. As he did it he glanced every now and then at Sara, just as the sparrows had done, and his expression was so apologetic that it touched her heart.

She sat and watched him without making any movement. One crumb was much larger than the others. It was evident that he wanted that piece, but it lay near the footstool and he was still rather timid. She scarcely allowed herself to breathe, she was so deeply interested. The rat shuffled a little nearer and ate a few more crumbs; then he stopped and sniffed delicately, giving a side glance at the occupant of the footstool. Then he darted at the piece of bun with something like the sudden boldness of the sparrow, and the instant he had possession of it fled back to the wall, slipped down a crack in the baseboard, and was gone.

"I knew he wanted it for his children," said Sara. "I do believe I could make friends with him."

A week or so afterward, on one of the rare nights when Ermengarde found it safe to steal up to the attic, when she tapped on the door with the tips of her fingers Sara did not

94

come to her for two or three minutes.

"There!" Ermengarde finally heard Sara say with a low laugh. "Take it and go home, Melchisedec! Go home to your wife!"

Almost immediately Sara opened the door for her.

"Who—who are you talking to, Sara?" she gasped.

Sara drew her in cautiously, but she looked as if something pleased and amused her.

"You must promise not to be frightened—not to scream the least bit, or I can't tell you," she answered.

Ermengarde felt inclined to scream on the spot, but managed to control herself. She looked all round the attic and saw no one. And yet Sara had been speaking to someone. She thought of ghosts.

"Is it—something that will frighten me?" she asked nervously.

"Some people are afraid of them," said Sara. "I was at first—but I am not now."

"Was it—a ghost?" quaked Ermengarde.

"No," said Sara, laughing. "It was my rat."

Ermengarde made one bound and landed in the middle of the dingy little bed. She tucked her feet under her nightgown and the red shawl. She did not scream, but she gasped with fright.

"Oh! Oh!" she cried under her breath. "A rat! A rat!"

"I was afraid you would be frightened," said Sara. "But you needn't be. I am making him tame. He actually knows me and comes out when I call him. Are you too frightened to want to see him?"

At first Ermengarde was too alarmed to do anything but huddle in a heap upon the bed, but the sight of Sara's composed little countenance and the story of Melchisedec's first appearance began at last to rouse her curiosity. She leaned forward over the edge of the bed and watched Sara go and kneel down by the hole in the baseboard.

"He—he won't run out quickly and jump on the bed, will he?"

"No," answered Sara. "He's as polite as we are. He is just like a person. Now watch!"

She began to make a low, whistling sound—so low and coaxing that it could only have been heard in entire stillness. She did it several times, looking entirely absorbed. And at last, evidently in response, a gray-whiskered, bright-eyed head peeped out of the hole. Sara had some crumbs in her hand. She dropped them, and Melchisedec came quietly forth and ate them. He took the largest piece and carried it in the most businesslike manner back to his home.

"You see," said Sara, "that is for his wife and children. He is very nice. He eats only the little bits. After he goes back I can always hear his family squeaking for joy. There are three kinds of squeaks. One kind is the children's, and one is Mrs. Melchisedec's, and one is Melchisedec's own."

Ermengarde began to laugh. "Oh, Sara!" she said. "You are strange—but you are nice."

"I know I am strange," admitted Sara cheerfully, "and I try to be nice." She rubbed her forehead, and a puzzled, tender look came into her face. "Papa always laughed at me," she said, "but I liked it. He thought I was strange, but he liked me to make up things. I—I can't help making up things. If I didn't, I don't believe I could live." She paused and glanced around the attic. "I'm sure I couldn't live here," she added in a low voice.

Ermengarde was interested, as she always was. "When you talk about things," she said, "they seem real. You talk about Melchisedec as if he was a person."

"He gets hungry and frightened, just as we do," said Sara, "and he is married and has children. How do we know he doesn't think things just as we do? His eyes look as if he was a person. That was why I gave him a name." She sat down on the floor, holding her knees.

"Besides," she said, "he is a Bastille rat sent to be my friend."

"Do you always pretend it is the Bastille?"

"Nearly always," answered Sara. "Sometimes I try to pretend it is another kind of place, but the Bastille is generally easiest—particularly when it is cold."

At that moment Ermengarde almost jumped off the bed, she was so startled by a sound she heard. It was like two distinct knocks on the wall.

"What is that?" she exclaimed.

Sara got up from the floor and answered dramatically, "It is the prisoner in the next cell."

"Becky!" cried Ermengarde.

"Yes," said Sara. "Listen—the two knocks meant 'Prisoner, are you there?' "

She knocked three times on the wall herself, in answer.

"That means, 'Yes, I am here, and all is well.' "

Four knocks came from Becky's side of the wall.

"That means," explained Sara, " 'Then, fellow-sufferer, we will sleep in peace. Good night.' "

Ermengarde beamed with delight.

"Oh, Sara!" she whispered joyfully. "It is like a story!"

"It is a story," said Sara. "*Everything's* a story. You are a story. I am a story. Miss Minchin is a story."

And she sat down again and talked until Ermengarde had to be reminded that she could not remain in the Bastille all night, but must steal noiselessly downstairs again and creep back into her deserted bed.

10

THE INDIAN GENTLEMAN

IT WAS A perilous thing for Ermengarde and Lottie to make pilgrimages to the attic. They could never be sure when Sara would be there in the daytime or when Miss Amelia might make a tour of inspection through the bedrooms at night. So their visits were rare.

Sara was lonelier when she was downstairs than when she was in her attic because she had no one to talk to. And when she walked through the streets, a forlorn little figure carrying a basket or a package, trying to hold her hat on when the wind was blowing and feeling the water soak through her shoes when it was raining, the crowds hurrying past made her feel even lonelier. When she had been the Princess Sara driving through the streets in her carriage or walking with Mariette, the sight of her bright, eager little face and pretty coats and hats had often caused people to smile at her. A happy, beautifully cared for little girl naturally attracts attention. Shabby, poorly dressed children are not rare enough and pretty enough to make people notice. No one seemed to see Sara as she hurried along the crowded pavements. Sometimes when she passed a shop window with a mirror in it, she almost laughed outright on catching a glimpse of herself, and sometimes her face went red and she bit her lip and turned away.

In the evening, when she passed houses whose windows were lighted up, she used to look into the warm rooms and amuse herself by imagining things about the people she saw there. There were several families in the square in which Miss Minchin lived. The one she liked best she called the Large Family because there were so many of them. There were eight children and a stout, rosy mother, and a stout, rosy father, and a stout, rosy grandmother, and any number of servants. The eight children were always being taken out by nursemaids to walk or to ride in baby buggies; or going for rides with their mamma; or flying to the door in the evening to meet their papa and kiss him and dance around him and drag off his overcoat and look in the pockets for packages; or crowding about the nursery windows and looking out and pushing each other and laughing. They were always doing something enjoyable. Sara was fond of them, and had given them romantic names out of books. She called them the Montmorencys. The fat, fair baby with the lace cap was Ethelberta Beauchamp Montmorency; the next baby was Violet Cholmondeley Montmorency; the little boy who had such round legs was Sydney Cecil Vivian Montmorency; and then came Lilian Evangeline Maud Marion, Rosalind Gladys, Guy Clarence, Veronica Eustacia, and Claude Harold Hector.

One evening a very funny thing happened, though in one sense it was not a funny thing at all.

Several of the Montmorency children were evidently going to a party, and just as Sara was about to pass the door, they were crossing the pavement to get into the waiting carriage. Veronica Eustacia and Rosalind Gladys, in white-lace frocks and lovely sashes, had just got in, and Guy Clarence, aged five, was following them. He was such a pretty fellow and had such rosy cheeks and blue eyes and such a darling little round head covered with curls that Sara forgot her basket and shabby cloak and paused and looked.

It was Christmas time, and the Large Family had been hearing many stories about children who were poor and had no mammas and papas to fill their stockings—children who were cold and thinly clad and hungry. In the stories, kind people— sometimes little boys and girls with tender hearts—invariably saw the poor children and gave them money or took them home to beautiful dinners. Guy Clarence burned with a desire to find such a poor child and give her a certain sixpence he possessed. An entire sixpence, he was sure, would mean wealth for evermore. As he crossed the strip of red carpet laid across the pavement from the door to the carriage, he had this very sixpence in his pocket. And just as Rosalind Gladys got into the vehicle and jumped on the seat in order to feel the cushions spring under her, he saw Sara standing on the wet pavement in her shabby frock and hat, with her old basket on her arm, looking at him hungrily.

He thought her eyes looked hungry because she had had nothing to eat for a long time. He did not know that she was hungry for the warm, merry life his home held, and that she had a hungry wish to snatch him in her arms and kiss him. He only knew that she had big eyes and a thin face and thin legs and poor clothes. So he put his hand in his pocket and found his sixpence and walked up to her kindly.

"Here, poor little girl," he said. "Here is a sixpence. I will give it to you."

Sara suddenly realized that she looked exactly like poor children she had seen in her better days. And she had given them pennies many a time. Her face went red and then it went pale, and for a second she felt as if she could not take the dear little sixpence.

"Oh, no!" she said. "Oh, no, thank you. I mustn't take it!"

Her voice was so unlike an ordinary street child's voice and her manner was so like the manner of a well-to-do person that Veronica Eustacia (whose real name was Janet) and Rosalind Gladys (who was really called Nora) leaned forward to listen.

But Guy Clarence was determined to do his good deed. He thrust the sixpence into her hand.

"Yes, you must take it, poor little girl!" he insisted. "You can buy things to eat with it. It is a whole sixpence!"

There was something so honest and kind in his face that Sara knew she must not refuse him. So she put her pride in her pocket, though her cheeks burned.

"Thank you," she said. "You are a kind, kind little darling thing." And as he scrambled joyfully into the carriage she went away, trying to smile, though she caught her breath quickly and her eyes were shining through a mist. She had known that she looked odd and shabby, but until now she had not known that she might be taken for a beggar.

As the Large Family's carriage drove away, the children inside it were talking with interested excitement.

"Oh, Donald," Janet exclaimed, "why did you offer that little girl your sixpence? I'm sure she is not a beggar! You know, it makes people angry to be taken for beggars when they are not beggars."

"She wasn't angry," said Donald, a trifle dismayed, but still firm. "She laughed a little, and she said I was a kind, kind little darling thing. And I was! It was my whole sixpence."

Janet and Nora exchanged glances.

"A beggar girl would never have said that," decided Janet.

"She would have said, 'Thank yer kindly, little gentleman—thank yer, sir'; and perhaps she would have bobbed a curtsy."

From that time on, the Large Family was as profoundly interested in Sara as she was in it. Faces used to appear at the nursery windows when she passed, and many discussions were held about her.

"She is a kind of servant at the girls' school," Janet said. "I believe she is an orphan. But she is not a beggar, however shabby she looks."

And afterward she was called by all of them, "The-little-girl-who-is-not-a-beggar," which was rather a long name, and sounded very funny when the youngest ones said it in a hurry.

Sara managed to bore a hole in the sixpence and hung it on an old bit of narrow ribbon round her neck. Her affection for the Large Family increased. She grew fonder and fonder of Becky, and she used to look forward to the two mornings a week when she went into the schoolroom to give the little ones their French lesson. Her small pupils loved her, and strove with each other for the privilege of standing close to her and slipping their small hands into hers. It fed her hungry heart to feel them nestling up to her. She made such friends with the sparrows that when she stood on the table, put her head and shoulders out of the attic window and chirped, she heard almost immediately a flutter of wings and answering twitters, and a little flock of dingy town birds appeared and alighted on the slates to talk to her and make much of the crumbs she scattered. Melchisedec actually brought Mrs. Melchisedec with him sometimes, and now and then one or two of his children. Sara used to talk to him, and somehow he looked as if he understood.

She would have liked to believe or pretend to believe that Emily understood and sympathized. She used to stare at her and pretend about her until her own eyes would grow large with something which was almost like fear—particularly at night when everything was so still, when the only sound in the attic was the occasional sudden scurry and squeak of Melchisedec's family in the wall. Sometimes after she had stared at Emily, Sara would ask her questions and find herself almost feeling as if she would presently answer. But she never did.

"As to answering, though," said Sara, trying to console herself, "I don't answer very often anymore. When people are insulting you, there is nothing so good for them as not to say a word—just to look at them and *think*. Miss Minchin turns pale with rage when I do it, Miss Amelia looks frightened, and so do the girls. When you will not fly into a passion, people know you are stronger than they are, because you are strong enough to hold in your rage and they are not, and they say stupid things they wish they hadn't said. There's nothing so strong as rage, except what makes you hold it in—that's stronger. It's a good thing not to answer your enemies. Perhaps Emily would rather not answer her friends, either. She keeps it all in her heart."

But though she tried to satisfy herself with these arguments, she did not find it easy. When, after a long, hard day, in which she had been sent here and there, sometimes on long errands through wind and cold and rain, she came in wet and hungry, and was sent out again because nobody chose to remember that she was only a child, and that her slim legs might be tired and her small body might be chilled; when she had been given only harsh words and cold looks for thanks; when the cook had been vulgar; when Miss Minchin had been in her worst mood and she had seen the girls sneering among themselves at her shabbiness—then she was not always able to comfort her sore, proud, desolate heart when Emily merely sat upright in her old chair and stared.

One of these nights, when she came up to the attic cold and hungry, Emily's stare seemed so vacant, her sawdust legs and arms so inexpressive, that Sara lost all control over herself. There was nobody but Emily—no one in the world. And there she sat.

"I shall die soon," she said at first.

Emily simply stared.

"I can't bear this," said the poor child, trembling. "I know I shall die. I'm cold, I'm wet, I'm starving to death. I've walked a thousand miles today, and they have done nothing but scold me from morning until night. And because I could not find that last thing the cook sent me for, they would not give me any supper. Some men laughed at me because my old shoes made me slip down in the mud. I'm covered with mud now. And they laughed. Do you hear!"

She looked at the staring glass eyes and complacent face, and suddenly a sort of heartbroken rage seized her. She lifted her little hand and knocked Emily off the chair, bursting into a passion of sobbing—Sara who never cried.

"You are nothing but a doll!" she cried. "Nothing but a doll-doll-doll! You care for nothing. You are stuffed with sawdust. You never had a heart. Nothing could ever make you feel. You are a doll!"

Emily lay on the floor, with her legs doubled up over her head, and a new flat place on the end of her nose. But she was calm, even dignified. Sara hid her face in her arms. The rats in the wall began to fight and bite each other and squeak and scramble. Melchisedec was punishing some of his family.

Sara's sobs gradually quieted themselves. It was so unlike her to break down that she was surprised at herself. After a while she raised her face and looked at Emily, who seemed to be gazing at her with a kind of glassy-eyed sympathy. Sara bent and picked her up. Remorse overtook her. She even smiled at her-self a very little smile.

"You can't help being a doll," she said with a resigned sigh, "any more than Lavinia and Jessie can help not having any sense. We are not all made alike. Perhaps you do your sawdust best." And she kissed her and shook her clothes straight, and put her back on her chair.

She had wished very much that someone would move into the empty house next door because of the attic window which was so near hers. It would be so nice to see it propped open someday and a head and shoulders poking out.

"I might begin by saying, 'Good morning,' and all sorts of things might happen. But, of course, it's not likely that anyone but servants would sleep there."

One morning, on turning the corner of the square after a visit to the grocer's, the butcher's, and the baker's, she saw, to her great delight, that a van full of furniture had stopped before the house next door. The front doors were thrown open, and men were going in and out carrying heavy packages and pieces of furniture.

"It's taken!" she said. "It really is taken! Oh, I do hope a nice head will look out of the attic window!"

She would have liked to watch some of the furniture being carried in so she could guess something about the people it belonged to.

"Miss Minchin's tables and chairs are just like her," she thought. "I remember thinking that the first minute I saw her, even though I was so little. I told Papa afterward, and he laughed and said it was true. I am sure the Large Family have fat, comfortable armchairs and sofas, and I can see that their red-flowery wallpaper is exactly like them. It's warm and cheer-ful and kind-looking and happy."

She was sent out for parsley to the greengrocer's later in the day, and when she came back several pieces of furniture had been set out of the van upon the pavement. There was a beautiful table of elaborately wrought teakwood, some chairs, and a screen covered with rich Oriental embroidery. The sight of them gave her a weird, homesick feeling. She had seen things so like them in India. One of the things Miss Minchin had taken from her was a carved teakwood desk her father had sent her.

"They are beautiful things," she said. "They look as if they ought to belong to a nice person. All the things look rather grand. I suppose it is a rich family."

The vans of furniture came and were unloaded and gave place to others all day. Several times Sara had an opportunity to see things carried in. All the furniture was rich and beautiful, and a great deal of it was Oriental. Wonderful rugs and draperies and ornaments were taken from the vans, many pictures, and books enough for a library.

"Someone in the family must have been in India," Sara thought. "I am glad. I shall feel as if they were friends, even if a head never looks out of the attic window."

When she was taking in the evening's milk for the cook (there was no odd job she was not called upon to do), she saw something that made the situation more interesting than ever. The handsome, rosy man who was the father of the Large Family walked across the square in the most matter-of-fact manner, and ran up the steps of the next-door house. He ran up them as if he felt quite at home and expected to run up and down them many a time in the future. He stayed inside a long time, and several times came out and gave directions to the workmen, as if he had a right to do so. It was clear that he was in charge.

"If the new people have children," Sara speculated, "the Large Family children will be sure to come and play with them, and they might come up into the attic just for fun."

At night after her work was done, Becky came in to see her fellow prisoner and bring her news.

"It's a' Nindian gentleman that's comin' to live next door, miss," she said. "I don't know whether he's a black gentleman or not, but he's a' Nindian one. He's very rich, an' he's ill, an' the gentleman of the Large Family is his lawyer. He's had a lot of trouble, an' it's made him ill an' low in his mind. He worships idols, miss. He's an 'eathen an' bows down to wood an' stone. I seen a' idol bein' carried in for him to worship. Somebody had oughter send him a tract. You can get a tract for a penny."

Sara laughed a little.

"I don't believe he worships idols," she said. "Some people like to keep figurines to look at because they are interesting."

But Becky preferred to believe that the new neighbor was "an 'eathen." It sounded so much more romantic than that he should merely be the ordinary kind of gentleman who went to church with a prayer book. She sat and talked long that night of what he would be like, of what his wife would be like if he had one, and of what his children would be like if they had children. Sara saw that Becky could not help hoping that they would all be black and would wear turbans and, above all, that they would all be " 'eathens."

"I never lived next door to no 'eathens, miss," she said. "I should like to see what sort o' ways they'd have."

It was several weeks before her curiosity was satisfied, and then it was revealed that the new occupant had neither wife nor children. A carriage drove up one day and stopped before the house. When the footman dismounted from the box and opened the door, the father of the Large Family got out first. After him came a nurse in uniform, then two men-servants, then a man with a haggard, distressed face, and a skeleton body wrapped in furs. He was carried up the steps, and the head of the Large Family went with him, looking very anxious. Shortly afterward a doctor's carriage arrived, and the doctor went in to take care of him.

"There is such a yellow gentleman next door, Sara," Lottie whispered at the French class afterward. "Do you think he is a Chinese? The geography book says Chinese men are yellow."

"No, he is not Chinese," Sara whispered back. "He is very ill. Go on with your lesson, Lottie."

That was the beginning of the story of the Indian gentleman.

11
RAM DASS

THERE WERE FINE sunsets sometimes. From the street, one could see only parts of them between the chimneys and over the roofs. From the kitchen windows one could not see them at all, and could only guess that they were going on because the bricks looked warm and the air rosy or yellow for a while. There was, however, a place from which one could see all the splendor: the piles of red or gold clouds in the west; or the purple ones edged with dazzling brightness; or the little fleecy, floating ones, tinged with rose-color and looking like flights of pink doves scurrying across the blue in a great hurry. The place where one could see all this was the attic window.

When the street suddenly began to glow in an enchanted way, Sara knew something was going on in the sky. When it was possible to leave the kitchen without being missed, she stole up the flights of stairs and climbed up on the old table to get her head and body as far out of the window as possible. When she had accomplished this, she always drew a long breath of fresh air and looked all round her. It was as if she had all the sky and the world to herself. Other attic skylights were usually closed, but even if they were propped open to let in air, no one seemed to come near them. And there Sara would stand, sometimes turning her face upward to the blue which seemed so friendly and near, just like a lovely vaulted ceiling; sometimes watching the west, the clouds melting or drifting or softly changing to pink or crimson or snow-white or purple or pale dove-gray. Sometimes they made islands or great mountains enclosing lakes of deep turquoise-blue, or liquid amber, or green; sometimes dark headlands jutted into strange, lost seas. There were places where it seemed that one could run or climb or stand and wait to see what next was coming—until, perhaps, as it all melted, one could float away. At least it seemed so to Sara, and nothing had ever been quite so beautiful to her as what she saw as she stood on the table—her body half out of the skylight—the sparrows twittering with sunset softness on the slate roof.

There was such a sunset as this a few days after the Indian gentleman was brought to his new home; and since the afternoon's work was done in the kitchen and nobody had ordered her to go anywhere or perform any task, Sara found it easier than usual to slip away and go upstairs.

She mounted her table and stood looking out. It was a wonderful moment. There were floods of molten gold covering the west, as if a glorious tide was sweeping over the world. A deep, rich yellow light filled the air; the birds flying across the tops of the houses showed quite black against it.

"It's a Splendid one," said Sara softly to herself. "It makes me feel almost afraid—as if something strange was just going to happen. The Splendid ones always make me feel like that."

She suddenly turned her head because she heard a sound a few yards away from her. It was an odd sound like a queer little squeaky chattering. It came from the window of the next attic. Someone had come to look at the sunset as she had. There was a head and a part of a body emerging from the skylight, but it was not the head or body of a little girl or a housemaid; it was the dark-faced, gleaming-eyed, white-turbaned head of a native Indian manservant. "A lascar," Sara said to herself quickly, and the sound she had heard came from a small monkey he held in his arms as if he were fond of it, and which was snuggling and chattering against his chest.

As Sara looked toward him he looked toward her. The first thing she thought was that his dark face looked homesick. She felt absolutely sure he had come up to look at the sun because he had seen it so seldom in England. She looked at him for a second and then smiled across the slates.

His whole expression altered, and he showed such gleaming white teeth as he smiled back that it was as if a light had been illuminated in his dusky face.

The monkey was impish and always ready for adventure, and it is probable that the sight of a little girl excited him. He suddenly broke loose, jumped on to the slates, ran across them chattering, and actually leaped on to Sara's shoulder and from there down into her attic room. It made her laugh, but she knew he must be restored to his master and she wondered how this was to be done.

She turned to the lascar, feeling glad that she still remembered some of the Hindustani she had learned when she lived with her father. She spoke to him in the language he knew.

"Will he let me catch him?" she asked.

She thought she had never seen more surprise and delight than the dark face expressed when she spoke in the familiar tongue. At once Sara saw that he had been accustomed to European children. He poured forth a flood of respectful thanks. The monkey was a good monkey and would not bite, but unfortunately, he was difficult to catch. He would flee from one spot to another like lightning. Ram Dass knew him as if he

111

His whole expression altered, and he showed such gleaming white teeth as he smiled back.

were his child, and Ram Dass he would sometimes obey, but not always. If Missee Sahib would permit Ram Dass, he himself could cross the roof to her room, enter the windows and regain the unworthy little animal. But he was evidently afraid Sara would not let him come.

Sara gave him permission at once. "Can you get across?"

"In a moment."

"Then come," she said. "He is flying from side to side of the room as if he is frightened."

Ram Dass slipped through his attic window and crossed to hers as steadily and lightly as if he had walked on roofs all his life. He slipped through the skylight and dropped upon his feet without a sound. Then he turned to Sara and bowed low. The monkey saw him and uttered a little scream. Ram Dass hastily took the precaution of shutting the skylight and then went in chase of him. It was not a very long chase. The monkey prolonged it a few minutes for the mere fun of it, but presently he sprang chattering on to Ram Dass's shoulder and sat there chattering and clinging to his neck with his weird little skinny arm.

Ram Dass thanked Sara profoundly. She had seen that his quick native eyes had taken in at a glance all the bare shabbiness of her room, but he spoke to her as if he were speaking to the daughter of a prince. This little evil one, he said, stroking the monkey, was in truth not so evil as he seemed; and his master, who was ill, was sometimes amused by him. He would have been sad if his favorite had run away and been lost. Then he bowed once more and got through the skylight and across the slates again with as much agility as the monkey himself.

When he had gone, Sara stood in the middle of her attic and thought of memories his face and costume and manner had brought back to her. It seemed a strange thing to remember that she—the drudge whom the cook had insulted an hour ago—had only a few years ago been surrounded by people who all treated her as Ram Dass had treated her—who bowed when she went by, whose foreheads almost touched the ground when she spoke to them, who were her servants. It was like a dream. It was all over, and it could never come back. She knew what Miss Minchin intended that her future should be. So long as she was too young to be used as a regular teacher, she would be used as an errand girl and servant. She was supposed to spend most evenings studying, and at various intervals she would be tested to make sure her education was advancing. Miss Minchin knew that Sara could learn without teachers. Give her books, and she would devour them and end by knowing them by heart. This was what would happen: when she was older she would be expected to drudge in the schoolroom as she drudged now everywhere else. They would give her plain and ugly teaching clothes. That was all there was to look forward to.

Then a thought came back to her which made the color rise in her cheek and a spark light itself in her eyes. She straightened her thin little body and lifted her head.

"Whatever comes," she said, "cannot alter one thing. If I am a princess in rags and tatters, I can be a princess inside. It would be easy to be a princess if I were dressed in cloth of gold, but it is a great deal more of a triumph to be one all the time when no one knows it. There was Marie Antoinette when she was in prison and her throne was gone and she had only a black gown on, and her hair was white, and they insulted her. She was a great deal more like a queen then than when she was so gay and everything was so grand. I like her best then. Those howling mobs of people did not frighten her. She was stronger than they were, even when they cut her head off."

This was not a new thought, but quite an old one by this

time. It had consoled her through many a bitter day, and she had gone about the house with an expression on her face that Miss Minchin could not understand and was a source of great annoyance to her. It was as if she scarcely heard the rude and acid things said to her; or if she heard them, did not care about them at all. Sometimes Miss Minchin would find Sara's eyes fixed upon her with something like a proud smile in them. At such times she did not know that Sara was saying to herself:

You don't know that you are saying these things to a princess, and that if I chose I could wave my hand and order you to execution. I only spare you because I am a princess, and you are a poor, unkind, vulgar old thing and don't know any better.

She found comfort in this and it was a good thing for her. While the thought held possession of her, she could not be made rude and malicious by the rudeness and malice of those about her.

"A princess must be polite," she said to herself.

And so when the servants, taking their tone from their mistress, were insolent and ordered her about, she would hold her head erect and reply to them with a quaint civility which often made them stare at her.

"She's got more airs and graces than if she come from Buckingham Palace, that young one," said the cook, chuckling a little sometimes. "I lose my temper with her often enough, but she never forgets her manners. 'If you please, cook,' 'Will you be so kind, cook?' 'I beg your pardon, cook.' She drops 'em about the kitchen as if they was nothing."

The morning after meeting Ram Dass and his monkey, Sara was in the schoolroom with her small pupils. Having finished giving them their lessons, she was putting the French exercise books together and thinking of the various things royal personages in disguise were called upon to do: Alfred the Great, for instance, burning the cakes and getting his ears boxed by a common housewife. How frightened she must have been when she found out who he was. If Miss Minchin should find out that she—Sara, whose toes were almost sticking out of her boots—was a princess—a real one! The look in her eyes was exactly the look Miss Minchin most disliked, and she saw it. She was so enraged that she suddenly boxed Sara's ears— exactly as the housewife had boxed King Alfred's. Sara wakened from her dream at the shock, and catching her breath, stood still a second. Then, not knowing she was going to do it, she broke into a little laugh.

"What are you laughing at, you impudent child?" Miss Minchin exclaimed.

Sara's cheeks were red and smarting from the blows.

"I was thinking," she answered.

"Apologize immediately!" said Miss Minchin. Sara hesitated a second before she replied.

"I will beg your pardon for laughing, if it was rude," she said. "But I won't beg your pardon for thinking."

"How dare you think! What were you thinking?"

Jessie tittered, and she and Lavinia nudged each other. All the girls looked up from their books to listen. It always interested them a little when Miss Minchin attacked Sara. Sara always said something queer and never seemed the least bit frightened. She was not in the least frightened now, though her boxed ears were scarlet and her eyes were as bright as stars.

"I was thinking," she answered grandly and politely, "that you did not know what you were doing."

"That I did not know what I was doing?" Miss Minchin fairly gasped.

"Yes," said Sara, "and I was thinking what would happen if I were a princess and you boxed my ears—what I should do to you. And I was thinking that if I were one, you would never dare to do it, whatever I said or did. And I was thinking how surprised and frightened you would be if you suddenly found out."

She had the imagined future so clearly before her eyes that she spoke in a manner that had an effect even upon Miss Minchin. It seemed for the moment to her narrow, unimaginative mind that there must be some real power hidden behind this candid daring.

"What?" Miss Minchin exclaimed. "Found out what?"

"That I really was a princess," said Sara, "and could do anything—anything I liked."

Every pair of eyes in the room widened to its full limit. Lavinia leaned forward on her seat to look.

"Go to your room this instant!" cried Miss Minchin, breathlessly. "Leave the schoolroom! Attend to your lessons, young ladies!"

Sara made a little bow.

"Excuse me for laughing if it was impolite," she said, and walked out of the room, leaving Miss Minchin struggling with her rage and the girls whispering over their books.

"Did you see her? Did you see how queer she looked?" Jessie broke out. "I shouldn't be at all surprised if she did turn out to be something. Suppose she should!"

12
THE OTHER SIDE OF THE WALL

WHEN ONE LIVES in a row of houses joined together, it is interesting to think of the things being done and said on the other side of the wall. Sara knew that the schoolroom was next to the Indian gentleman's study, and she hoped that the wall was thick so that the noise made sometimes after lesson hours would not disturb him.

"I am growing quite fond of him," she said to Ermengarde. "I should not like him to be disturbed. I have adopted him for a friend. You can do that with people you never speak to at all. You can just watch them and think about them and be sorry for them, until they seem almost like relatives."

"I have very few relatives," said Ermengarde, reflectively, "and I'm very glad of it. I don't like those I have. My two aunts are always saying, 'Dear me, Ermengarde! You are very fat. You shouldn't eat sweets,' and my uncle is always asking me things like, 'When did Edward the Third ascend the throne?' and, 'Who died of a surfeit of lampreys?' "

Sara laughed.

"People you never speak to can't ask you questions like that," she said. "And I'm sure the Indian gentleman wouldn't even if he was quite familiar with you. I am fond of him."

She had become fond of the Large Family because they looked happy, but she had become fond of the Indian gentleman because he looked unhappy. The servants in the school kitchen often discussed his case. He was not an Indian gentleman really, but an Englishman who had lived in India. He had met with great misfortunes that had for a time so imperiled his whole fortune that he had thought himself ruined and disgraced forever. The shock had been so great that he almost died of brain fever, and ever since he had been shattered in health, though his fortunes had changed and all his possessions had been restored to him. His trouble and peril had been connected with mines.

"And mines with diamonds in 'em!" said the cook. "None of my savin's goes into no mines—particular diamond ones"—with a side glance at Sara. "We all know somethin' of *them*."

"He felt as my papa felt," Sara thought. "He was ill as my papa was; but he did not die."

So her heart was more drawn to him than before. When she was sent out at night she was sometimes glad, because there was always a chance that the curtains of the house next door might not yet be closed and she could look into the warm room and see her adopted friend. She sometimes would stop and, holding to the iron railings, wish him good night as if he could hear her.

"Perhaps kind thoughts reach people somehow, even through windows and doors and walls. Perhaps you feel a little warm and comforted, and don't know why, when I am standing here in the cold and hoping you will get well and happy again. I am so sorry for you," she would whisper in an intense little voice. "Good night—good night. God bless you!"

She would go away, feeling comforted and a little warmer herself. Her sympathy was so strong that it seemed as if it *must* reach him somehow as he sat alone in his armchair by the fire, nearly always with his forehead resting in his hand as he gazed hopelessly into the fire.

"He always seems as if he were thinking of something that hurts him," she said to herself, "but he has his money back and he will get over his brain fever in time, so he ought not to look like that. I wonder if there is something else."

If there was something else—something even servants did not hear of—the father of the Large Family must know it, the gentleman she called Mr. Montmorency. Mr. Montmorency went to see him often, and Mrs. Montmorency and all the little Montmorencys went too, though less often. He seemed particularly fond of the two elder little girls—the Janet and Nora who had been so alarmed when their brother had given Sara his sixpence. Janet and Nora were as fond of him as he was of them, and looked forward to the afternoons when they were allowed to cross the square and make their well-behaved little visits to him.

"He is a poor thing," said Janet, "and he says we cheer him up. We try to cheer him up very quietly."

It was Janet who decided when it was right to ask him to tell stories about India, and it was she who saw when he was tired and it was the time to steal quietly away and tell Ram Dass to go to him. They were very fond of Ram Dass. He could have told any number of stories if he had been able to speak anything but Hindustani. The Indian gentleman's real name was Mr. Carrisford, and Janet told Mr. Carrisford about the encounter with the little-girl-who-was-not-a-beggar. He was very much interested, and all the more so when he heard from Ram Dass of the adventure of the monkey on the roof. Ram Dass described the attic and its desolateness—the bare floor and broken plaster, the rusty, empty grate, and the hard, narrow bed.

"Carmichael," the invalid said to the father of the Large Family, after he had heard this description, "I wonder how many of the attics in this square are like that one, and how many wretched little servant girls sleep on such beds, while I toss on my down pillows, loaded and harassed by wealth that is, most of it, not mine."

"My dear fellow," Mr. Carmichael answered cheerily, "the sooner you cease tormenting yourself the better it will be for you. If you possessed all the wealth of all the Indies, you could not set right all the discomforts in the world, and if you began to refurnish all the attics in this square, there would still remain all the attics in all the other squares and streets to fix. And there you are!"

Mr. Carrisford sat and bit his nails as he looked into the glowing bed of coals in the grate.

"Do you suppose," he said slowly, after a pause—"do you think it is possible that the other child—the child I never cease thinking of—could be—could possibly be reduced to any such condition as the poor little soul next door?"

Mr. Carmichael looked at him uneasily. He knew that the worst thing the man could do for himself was to begin to think in this particular way of this particular subject.

"If the child at Madame Pascal's school in Paris was the one you are in search of," he answered soothingly, "she would seem to be in the hands of people who can afford to take care of her. They adopted her because she had been the favorite companion of their little daughter who died. They had no other children, and Madame Pascal said that they were extremely well-to-do Russians."

"And the wretched woman actually did not know where they had taken her!" exclaimed Mr. Carrisford.

Mr. Carmichael shrugged his shoulders.

"Women of her type do not trouble themselves about the futures of children who might prove burdens. The adopted parents apparently disappeared and left no trace."

"But you say *if* the child was the one I am in search of. We are not sure. There was a difference in the name."

"Madame Pascal pronounced it as if it were Carew instead of Crewe—but that might be merely a matter of pronunciation. The circumstances were curiously similar. An English officer in India had placed his motherless little girl at the school. He had died suddenly after losing his fortune." Mr. Carmichael paused a moment, as if a new thought had occurred to him. "Are you sure the child was left at a school in Paris? Are you sure it was Paris?"

"My dear fellow," broke forth Carrisford, with restless bitterness, "I am sure of nothing. I never saw either the child or her mother. Ralph Crewe and I were boyhood friends, but we had not met since our school days, until we met in India. I was absorbed in the mines. He became absorbed, too. The whole thing was so huge and glittering that we half lost our heads. When we met we scarcely spoke of anything else. I only knew that the child had been sent to school somewhere."

He was beginning to be excited. He always became excited when his still weakened brain was stirred by memories of catastrophes.

Mr. Carmichael watched him anxiously. It was necessary to ask some questions, but they must be put quietly and with caution.

"But you had reason to think the school was in Paris."

"Yes," was the answer, "because her mother was a Frenchwoman, and wished her child to be educated in Paris. It seemed only likely that she would be there."

"Yes," Mr. Carmichael said, "it seems more than probable."

122

The Indian gentleman leaned forward and struck the table with a long, thin hand.

"Carmichael," he said, "I must find her. If she is friendless and penniless, it is my fault. How is a man to get well with a thing like that on his mind? This sudden change of luck at the mines has made realities of all our most fantastic dreams, and poor Crewe's child may be begging in the street!"

"No, no," said Carmichael. "Try to be calm. Console yourself with the fact that when she is found you have a fortune to hand over to her."

"Why was I not man enough to stand my ground when things looked black? Poor Crewe had put into the scheme every penny that he owned. He trusted me. And he died thinking I had ruined him—I—Tom Carrisford, who played cricket at Eton with him. What a villain he must have thought me!"

"Don't reproach yourself so bitterly."

"I reproach myself for losing my courage. I ran away like a swindler and a thief, because I could not face my best friend and tell him I had ruined him and his child."

The good-hearted father of the Large Family put his hand on his shoulder comfortingly.

"You were half delirious already. If you had not been you would have stayed and fought it. You were in a hospital, strapped down in bed, raving with brain fever, two days after you left. Remember that."

Carrisford dropped his forehead in his hands.

"Yes," he said. "I was driven mad with dread and horror. I had not slept for weeks. The night I staggered out of my house all the air seemed full of hideous things mocking me."

"That is explanation enough in itself," said Mr. Carmichael. "How could a man on the verge of brain fever judge sanely?"

Carrisford shook his drooping head.

"And when I returned to consciousness poor Crewe was dead and buried. And I seemed to remember nothing. I did not remember the child for months and months. Even when I began to recall her existence everything seemed in a sort of haze."

He stopped a moment and rubbed his forehead. "Surely I must sometime have heard Crewe speak of the school she was sent to. Don't you think so?"

"He might not have spoken of it definitely. You never seem even to have heard her real name."

"He used to call her his 'Little Missus.' But the wretched mines drove everything else out of our heads. We talked of nothing else. If he spoke of the school, I forgot—I forgot. And now I shall never remember."

"Come, come," said Carmichael. "We shall find her yet. Madame Pascal seemed to have a vague idea that the good-natured Russians lived in Moscow. We will take that as a clue. I will go to Moscow."

"If I were able to travel, I would go with you," said Carrisford, "but I can only sit here wrapped in furs and stare at the fire. And when I look into it I seem to see Crewe's face asking me a question. Sometimes I dream of him at night, and he always stands before me and asks the question. Can you guess what he says, Carmichael?"

Mr. Carmichael answered him in a rather low voice. "Not exactly."

"He always says, 'Tom, old man—Tom—where is the Little Missus?' " He caught at Carmichael's hand and clung to it. "I must be able to answer him—I must! Help me to find her. Help me."

On the other side of the wall Sara was sitting in her attic room talking to Melchisedec, who had come out for his evening meal.

"It has been hard to be a princess today, Melchisedec," she said. "It gets harder as the weather grows colder and the streets get more sloppy. When Lavinia laughed at my muddy skirt as I passed her in the hall, I thought of something to say—and I only just stopped myself in time. You can't sneer back at people like that if you are a princess. But you have to bite your tongue to hold yourself in. It was a cold afternoon, Melchisedec. And it's a cold night."

Quite suddenly she put her black head down in her arms, as she often did when she was alone.

"Oh, Papa," she whispered, "what a long time it seems since I was your 'Little Missus'!"

This was what happened that day on both sides of the wall.

13

ONE OF THE POPULACE

THE WINTER WAS a wretched one. There were days Sara tramped through snow when she went on her errands; there were worse days when the snow melted and combined with mud to form slush; there were others when the fog was so thick that the lamps in the street were lighted all day. On such days the windows of the house of the Large Family always looked delightfully cozy, and the study in which the Indian gentleman sat glowed with warmth and rich color. But the attic was dismal beyond words. There were no longer sunsets or sunrises to look at, and scarcely ever any stars. The clouds hung low over the skylight and were either gray or mud-color or dropping heavy rain. At four o'clock in the afternoon the daylight was at an end. If it was necessary to go to her attic for anything, Sara was obliged to light a candle. The women in the kitchen were depressed, and that made them more ill-tempered than ever. Becky was treated like a slave.

" 'Twarn't for you, miss," she said hoarsely to Sara one night when she had crept into the attic, " 'twarn't for you, an' the Bastille, an' bein' the prisoner in the next cell, I should die. The missus is more like the head jailer every day she lives. Tell me some more, please, miss—tell me about the subt'ranean passage we've dug under the walls."

"I'll tell you something warmer," shivered Sara. "Get your coverlet and wrap it round you, and I'll get mine, and we will huddle close together on the bed, and I'll tell you about the tropical forest where the Indian gentleman's monkey used to live. When I see him sitting on the table near the window and looking out into the street with that mournful expression, I always feel sure he is thinking about the tropical forest where he used to swing by his tail from coconut trees. I wonder who caught him and if he left a family behind who had depended on him for coconuts."

"That is warmer, miss," said Becky. "Someways even the Bastille is sort of heatin' when you gets to tellin' about it."

"That is because it makes you think of something else," said Sara, wrapping the coverlet round her until only her small face was to be seen looking out of it. "What you have to do with your mind when your body is miserable is to make it think of something else."

"Can you do it, miss?" faltered Becky.

Sara knitted her brows a moment. "Sometimes I can and sometimes I can't. But when I *can* I'm all right. I've been practicing a good deal lately, and it's beginning to be easier than it used to be. When things are horrible—just horrible—I think as hard as ever I can of being a princess."

One of the strongest tests she was ever put to came on a certain dreadful day which, she often thought afterward, would never fade out of her memory even in the years to come.

For several days it had rained continuously. The streets were chilly and sloppy and full of cold mist. There was mud everywhere—sticky London mud—and over everything the pall of drizzle and fog. Sara was sent out on errands again and again, until her shabby clothes were damp through. The absurd old feathers on her forlorn hat were more draggled and absurd than ever, and her downtrodden shoes were so wet they could not hold any more water. Added to this, she had been deprived of her dinner because Miss Minchin had chosen to punish her. She was so cold and hungry and tired that her face began to have a pinched look, and now and then some kind-hearted person passing her in the street glanced at her with sudden sympathy.

She hurried on, trying to make her mind think of something else. "Suppose I had dry clothes on," she thought. "Suppose I had good shoes and a long, thick coat and woolen stockings and a whole umbrella. And suppose—suppose—just when I was near a baker's where they sold hot buns, I should find six-pence—which belonged to nobody. Suppose, if I did, I should go into the shop and buy six of the hottest buns and eat them all without stopping."

Some very odd things happen in this world sometimes.

It certainly was an odd thing that happened to Sara. She had to cross the street just when she was saying this to herself. The mud was dreadful—she almost had to wade. She had to look down at her feet and the mud, and in looking down—just as she reached the pavement—she saw something shining in the gutter. It was actually a piece of silver—a tiny piece trodden upon by many feet, but still with spirit enough left to shine a little. Not quite a sixpence, but the next thing to it—a fourpenny piece.

In one second it was in her cold little red-and-blue hand.

"Oh," she gasped, "it is true! It is true!"

And then, if you will believe me, she looked straight at the shop directly facing her. It was a baker's shop, and a cheerful, stout, motherly woman with rosy cheeks was putting into the window a tray of delicious newly baked hot buns, fresh from the oven—large, plump, shiny buns, with currants in them.

It almost made Sara feel faint—the shock, and the sight of the buns, and the delightful odors of warm bread floating up through the baker's cellar window.

She knew the little piece of money had evidently been lying in the mud for some time, and its owner was completely lost in the stream of passing people who crowded and jostled each other all day long.

"But I'll go and ask the baker woman if she has lost anything," she said to herself, rather faintly. So she crossed the pavement and put her wet foot on the step. As she did so she saw something that made her stop.

It was a little figure more forlorn even than herself—a little figure who was not much more than a bundle of rags, from which small, bare, red, muddy feet peeped out because the rags their owner was trying to cover them with were not long enough. Above the rags appeared a shock head of tangled hair and a dirty face with big, hollow, hungry eyes.

"This," Sara said to herself with a little sigh, "is one of the populace—and she is hungrier than I am."

The child stared up at Sara and shuffled herself aside a little. She was used to getting out of the way. She knew that if a policeman chanced to see her he would tell her to move on.

Sara clutched her little fourpenny piece and hesitated for a few seconds. Then she spoke to her.

"Are you hungry?" she asked.

The child shuffled herself and her rags a little more. "Ain't I jist!" she said in a hoarse voice.

"Haven't you had any dinner?" said Sara.

"No dinner," more hoarsely still and with more shuffling. "Nor yet no bre'fast—nor yet no supper. No nothin'."

"Since when?" asked Sara.

"Dunno. Never got nothin' today—nowhere. I've axed an' axed."

"If I'm a princess," Sara said to herself, "if I'm a princess—when they were poor and driven from their thrones they always shared with the populace if they met one poorer and hungrier than themselves. They always shared. Buns are a penny each. If it had been sixpence I could have eaten six. It won't be enough for either of us. But it will be better than nothing."

"Wait a minute," she said to the beggar child.

She went into the shop. It was warm and smelled deliciously. The woman was just going to put some more hot buns into the window.

"If you please," said Sara, "have you lost fourpence—a silver fourpence?" And she held the forlorn little piece of money out to her.

The woman looked at it and then at her—at her intense little face and draggled, once fine clothes.

"Bless us, no," she answered. "Did you find it?"

"Yes," said Sara. "In the gutter."

"Keep it, then," said the woman. "It may have been there for a week, and goodness knows who lost it."

"I know that," said Sara, "but I thought I would ask you."

"Not many would," said the woman, looking puzzled and interested and good-natured all at once.

"Do you want to buy something?" she added, as she saw Sara glance at the buns.

"Four buns, if you please," said Sara. "Those at a penny each."

The woman went to the window and put some in a paper bag.

Sara noticed that she put in six.

130

"I said four, if you please," she explained. "I have only fourpence."

"I'll throw in two for makeweight," said the woman with her good-natured look. "I dare say you can eat them sometime. Aren't you hungry?"

A mist rose before Sara's eyes.

"Yes," she answered. "I am very hungry, and I am much obliged to you for your kindness, and—" She was going to add, "there is a child outside who is hungrier than I am." But just at that moment two or three customers came in at once, and each one seemed in a hurry, so she could only thank the woman again and go out.

The beggar girl was still huddled up in the corner of the step. She looked frightful in her wet and dirty rags. She was staring straight before her with an empty look of suffering, and she rubbed away the tears that forced their way from under her lids. She was muttering to herself.

Sara opened the paper bag and took out one of the hot buns, which had already warmed her own cold hands a little.

"See," she said, putting the bun in the ragged lap, "this is nice and hot. Eat it, and you will not feel so hungry."

The child stared up at her as if such sudden amazing good luck almost frightened her. Then she snatched up the bun and began to cram it into her mouth with great wolfish bites.

"Oh, my! Oh, my!" Sara heard her say hoarsely, in wild delight. Sara took out two more buns and put them down.

The sound in the hoarse, ravenous voice was awful.

"She is hungrier than I am," Sara said to herself. "She's starving." But her hand trembled when she put down the fourth bun. "I'm not starving," she said, and she put down the fifth.

The child was too ravenous to give any thanks, even if she had ever been taught politeness—which she had not. She was

*The child was too ravenous to give any thanks, even if she
had ever been taught politeness—which she had not.*

132

only a poor little London wild animal.

"Goodbye," said Sara.

When she reached the other side of the street she looked back. The child had a bun in each hand and had stopped in the middle of a bite to watch her. Sara gave her a little nod, and the child, after another stare—a curious lingering stare—jerked her shaggy head in response, and until Sara was out of sight she did not take another bite or even finish the one she had begun.

At that moment the baker-woman looked out of her shop window.

"Well, I never!" she exclaimed. "If that young un' hasn't given her buns to a beggar child! It wasn't because she didn't want them, either. I'd give something to know what she did it for."

She stood behind her window for a few moments and pondered. Then her curiosity got the better of her. She went to the door and spoke to the beggar child.

"Who gave you those buns?" she asked her.

The child nodded her head toward Sara's vanishing figure.

"What did she say?" inquired the woman.

"Axed me if I was 'ungry," replied the hoarse voice.

"What did you say?"

"Said I was jist."

"And then she came in and got the buns, and gave them to you, did she?"

The child nodded.

"How many?"

"Five."

The woman thought it over. "Left just one for herself," she said in a low voice. "And she could have eaten the whole six—I saw it in her eyes."

She looked after the little draggled far-away figure and felt more disturbed in her usually comfortable mind than she had felt for many a day.

"I wish she hadn't gone so quick," she said. "I'm blest if she shouldn't have had a dozen." Then she turned to the child.

"Are you hungry still?" she said.

"I'm allus hungry," was the answer, "but 't ain't as bad as it was."

"Come in here," said the woman, and she held open the shop door.

The child got up and shuffled in. To be invited into a warm place full of bread seemed an incredible thing. She did not know what was going to happen. She did not care.

"Get yourself warm," said the woman, pointing to a fire in the tiny back room. "And look here; when you are hard up for a bit of bread, you can come in here and ask for it. I'm blest if I won't give it to you for that young one's sake."

Sara found some comfort in her remaining bun. It was very hot, and it was better than nothing. As she walked along she broke off small pieces and ate them slowly to make them last longer.

"Suppose it was a magic bun," she said, "and a bite was as much as a whole dinner. I should be overeating myself if I went on like this."

It was dark when she reached the square where the Select Seminary was situated. The lights in the houses were all lighted. The blinds were not yet drawn in the windows of the room where she nearly always caught glimpses of members of the Large Family. Frequently at this hour she could see the gentleman she called Mr. Montmorency sitting in a big chair, with a small swarm round him talking, laughing, perching on the arms of his seat or on his knees or leaning against them. This evening the swarm was about him, but it was evident that a journey was to be taken, and it was Mr. Montmorency who was to take it. A carriage stood before the door, and a big trunk had been strapped upon it. The children were dancing about, chattering and hanging on to their father. The pretty rosy mother was standing near him, talking as if she was asking final questions. Sara paused a moment to see the little ones lifted up and kissed and the bigger ones bent over and kissed also.

"I wonder if he will stay away long," she thought. "The trunk is rather big. Oh dear, how they will miss him! I shall miss him myself—even though he doesn't know I am alive."

When the door opened she saw him come out and stand before the warmly-lighted hall, the older children still hovering about him.

"Will Moscow be covered with snow?" said Janet. "Will there be ice everywhere?"

"Shall you see the Czar?" cried another.

"I will write and tell you all about it," he answered, laughing. "I would rather stay with you than go to Moscow. Good night! Good night, duckies! God bless you!" And he ran down the steps and jumped into the carriage.

"If you find the little girl, give her our love," shouted Guy Clarence, jumping up and down on the door mat. Then they went in and shut the door.

"Did you see?" said Janet to Nora. "The little-girl-who-is-not-a-beggar was passing! She looked all cold and wet, and I saw her turn and look at us. Mamma says her clothes always look as if they had been given to her by someone who was quite rich. The people at the school always send her out on errands on the horridest days and nights."

Sara crossed the square to Miss Minchin's steps, feeling faint and shaky.

"I wonder who the little girl is," she thought, "the little girl he is going to look for."

And she went down the steps, lugging her heavy basket, as the father of the Large Family drove quickly on his way to the train station on his way to Moscow, where he was to search for the little lost daughter of Captain Crewe.

14

WHAT MELCHISEDEC HEARD AND SAW

ON THIS VERY afternoon, while Sara was out, a strange thing happened in the attic. Only Melchisedec saw and heard it; and he was so much alarmed and mystified that he scuttled back to his hole and hid there and peeped out to watch what was going on.

The attic had been very still after Sara left it in the early morning, the stillness broken only by the pattering of the rain upon the slates and the skylight. When the rain ceased to patter and perfect silence reigned, Melchisedec decided to come out and scout around, though experience taught him that Sara would not return for some time. He had been rambling and sniffing about and had just found a totally unexpected and unexplained crumb left from his last meal, when his attention was attracted by a sound on the roof. He stopped to listen with a palpitating heart. The sound suggested that something was moving on the roof. It was approaching the skylight; it reached the skylight. The skylight was being opened. A dark face peered into the attic; then another face appeared behind it, and both looked in. One was Ram Dass and the other was the Indian gentleman's secretary; but of course Melchisedec did not know this. He only knew that the men were invading the silence and privacy of the attic. And as the one with the dark face let himself down through the opening with such lightness and dexterity that he did not make the slightest sound, Melchisedec turned tail and fled back to his hole. He was frightened to death. He lay close and flat near the entrance of his home, just managing to peep through the crack with a bright, alarmed eye. How much he understood of the talk he heard I am not able to say.

The secretary, who was light and young, slipped through the skylight as noiselessly as Ram Dass had done. He caught a last glimpse of Melchisedec's vanishing tail.

"Was that a rat?" he asked Ram Dass in a whisper.

"Yes, a rat, sahib," answered Ram Dass, also whispering. "There are many in the walls."

"Ugh!" exclaimed the young man. "It is a wonder if the child is not terrified of them."

"The child is the little friend of all things, sahib," Ram Dass answered. "She is not as other children. I see her when she does not see me. I slip across the slates and look at her many nights to see that she is safe. I watch her from my window when she does not know I am near. She stands on the table there and looks out at the sky as if it spoke to her. The sparrows come at her call. The rat she has fed and tamed in her loneliness. The poor slave of the house comes to her for comfort. There is a little child who comes to her in secret; there is one older who worships her and would listen to her forever if she might. This I have seen when I have crept across the roof. By the mistress of the house—who is an evil woman—she is treated like an outcast. But she has the bearing of a child who is of the blood of kings!"

"You seem to know a great deal about her," the secretary said.

"All her life each day I know," answered Ram Dass. "Her

going out I know, and her coming in; her sadness and her poor joys; her coldness and her hunger. I know when she is alone until midnight, learning from her books. I know when her secret friends steal to her and she may laugh and talk with them in whispers."

"You are sure no one comes near this place but herself, and that she will not return and surprise us? She would be frightened if she found us here, and the Sahib Carrisford's plan would be spoiled."

Ram Dass crossed noiselessly to the door and stood close to it.

"None mount here but herself, sahib," he said. "She has gone out with her basket and may be gone for hours. If I stand here I can hear any step before it reaches the last flight of the stairs."

The secretary took a pencil and a tablet from his breast pocket.

"Keep your ears open," he said, and he began to walk slowly and softly round the miserable little room, making rapid notes on his tablet as he looked at things.

First he went to the narrow bed. He pressed his hand upon the mattress and uttered an exclamation.

"As hard as a stone," he said. "That will have to be altered some day when she is out. A special journey can be made to bring it across. It cannot be done tonight." He lifted the covering and examined the one thin pillow.

"Coverlet dingy and worn, blanket thin, sheets patched and ragged," he said. "What a bed for a child to sleep in—and in a house which calls itself respectable! There has not been a fire in that grate for many a day," glancing at the rusty fireplace.

"Never since I have seen it," said Ram Dass. "The mistress of the house is not one who remembers that another than herself may be cold."

The secretary was writing quickly on his tablet. He looked up from it as he tore off a leaf and slipped it into his breast pocket.

"This is a strange way of doing the thing. Who planned it?"

Ram Dass bowed modestly.

"It is true that the first thought was mine, sahib," he said. "Being sad one night, I lay close to the open skylight and listened to her talk to a friend. The vision she related told what this miserable room might be if it had comforts in it. She seemed to see it as she talked, and she grew cheered and warmed as she spoke. The next day, the sahib being ill and wretched, I told him of the thing to amuse him. To hear of the child's doings gave him entertainment. He became interested in her and asked questions. At last he began to please himself with the thought of making her visions real things."

"You think that it can be done while she sleeps? Suppose she awakened," suggested the secretary; and it was evident that the plan had caught his fancy as well as Carrisford's.

"I can move as if my feet were of velvet," Ram Dass replied, "and children sleep soundly—even the unhappy ones. I could have entered this room in the night many times without causing her to turn upon her pillow. When she awakens she will think a magician has been here."

He smiled as if his heart warmed under his white robe, and the secretary smiled back at him.

"It will be like a story from the *Arabian Nights*," he said. "Only an Oriental could have planned it. It does not belong to London fogs."

They did not remain very long, to the great relief of Melchisedec. The young secretary wrote down things about the floor, the fireplace, the broken footstool, the old table, the walls—which last he touched with his hand again and again, seeming much pleased when he found that a number of old nails had been driven in various places.

"Yesterday, when she was out," Ram Dass said, "I entered, bringing with me small, sharp nails which can be pressed into the wall without blows from a hammer. I placed many in the plaster where I may need them."

The Indian gentleman's secretary stood still and looked round him as he thrust his tablets back into his pocket.

"I think I have made notes enough; we can go now," he said. "Mr. Carrisford has a warm heart. It is a thousand pities that he has not found the lost child."

"If he should find her his strength would be restored to him," said Ram Dass. "His God may lead her to him yet."

Then they slipped through the skylight as noiselessly as they had entered it. After he was sure they had gone, Melchisedec felt it safe to emerge from his hole again and scuffle about in the hope that even such alarming human beings as these might have carried crumbs in their pockets and dropped one or two of them.

15
PROVIDENCE

WHEN SARA HAD passed the house next door that evening, she saw Ram Dass closing the shutters to a nice room with a bright fire glowing in the grate and the Indian gentleman sitting before it with his head in his hand.

"Poor man!" said Sara. "I wonder what you are supposing."

And this was what he was "supposing" at that very moment.

"Suppose," he was thinking, "suppose—even if Carmichael traces the people to Moscow—the little girl they took from Madame Pascal's school in Paris is not the one we are in search of. What steps shall I take next?"

When Sara went into the house she met Miss Minchin, who had come downstairs to scold the cook.

"Where have you wasted your time?" she demanded. "You have been out for hours."

"It was so wet and muddy," Sara answered, "it was hard to walk, because my shoes were so bad and slipped about."

"Make no excuses," said Miss Minchin, "and tell no falsehoods."

Sara went in to the cook. The cook had received a severe lecture and was in a fearful temper as a result. She was only too rejoiced to have someone to vent her rage on.

"Why didn't you stay all night?" she snapped.

Sara laid her purchases on the table.

"Here are the things," she said.

The cook looked them over, grumbling.

"May I have something to eat?" Sara asked rather faintly.

"Tea's over and done with," was the answer. "Did you expect me to keep it hot for you?"

Sara stood silent for a second.

"I had no dinner," she said next, and her voice was quite low. She made it low because she was afraid it would tremble.

"There's some bread in the pantry," said the cook. "That's all you'll get at this time of day."

Sara went and found the hard, dry bread. The cook was in too vicious a humor to give her anything to eat with it. It was hard for Sara to climb the three long flights of stairs to her attic. She often found them long and steep when she was tired, but tonight it seemed as if she would never reach the top. Several times she had to stop to rest. When she reached the top landing, she was glad to see a glimmer of light coming from under her door. That meant that Ermengarde had managed to creep up to pay her a visit. The mere presence of plump, comfortable Ermengarde, wrapped in her red shawl, would warm it a little.

Yes, there Ermengarde was, sitting in the middle of the bed with her feet tucked safely under her. She had never become friendly with Melchisedec and his family, though they fascinated her. On this occasion she had become rather nervous because Melchisedec had appeared and sniffed about a good deal, and once sat up on his hind legs and looked at her, sniffing pointedly in her direction.

"Oh, Sara," she cried out, "I am glad you have come. I like Melchy, you know, but it does frighten me when he sniffs right at me. Do you think he ever would jump?"

"No," answered Sara.

Ermengarde crawled forward on the bed to look at her. "You look tired, Sara," she said. "You are quite pale."

"I *am* tired," said Sara, dropping on to the lopsided footstool. "Oh, there's Melchisedec, poor thing. He's come to ask for his supper."

He came forward with an affectionate, expectant expression as Sara put her hand in her pocket and turned it inside out, shaking her head.

"I'm very sorry," she said. "I haven't one crumb left. Go home, Melchisedec, and tell your wife there was nothing in my pocket. I'm afraid I forgot because the cook and Miss Minchin were so cross."

Melchisedec seemed to understand.

"I did not expect to see you tonight, Ermie," Sara said. Ermengarde hugged herself in the red shawl.

"Miss Amelia has gone out to spend the night with her old aunt," she explained. "No one else ever comes and looks into the bedrooms after we are in bed. I could stay here until morning if I wanted to."

She pointed toward a pile of books on the table under the skylight.

"Papa has sent me some more books, Sara," she said. "There they are."

Sara ran to the table, and picking up the top volume, turned over its leaves quickly. For the moment she forgot her discomforts.

"Ah," she cried out, "how beautiful! Carlyle's *French Revolution*. I have so wanted to read that!"

"I haven't," said Ermengarde. "And Papa will be so cross if I don't. He'll expect me to know all about it when I go home for the holidays. What shall I do?"

Sara stopped turning the pages and looked at her with an excited flush on her cheeks.

"Look here," she cried, "if you'll lend me these books, *I'll* read them—and tell you everything that's in them afterward—and I'll tell it so that you will remember it, too."

"Oh, goodness!" exclaimed Ermengarde. "Do you think you can?"

"I know I can," Sara answered. "The little ones always remember what I tell them."

"Sara," said Ermengarde, hope gleaming in her round face, "if you'll do that, and make me remember, I'll—I'll give you anything."

"I don't want you to give me anything," said Sara. "I want your books!" And her eyes grew big, and her chest heaved.

"Take them, then," said Ermengarde. "I wish I wanted them—but I don't. I'm not clever, and my father is, and he thinks I ought to be."

Sara was opening one book after the other. "What are you going to tell your father?" she asked, a slight doubt dawning in her mind.

"Oh, he needn't know," answered Ermengarde. "He'll think I've read them."

Sara put down her book and shook her head slowly. "That's almost like telling lies," she said. "And lies—well, you see, they are not only wicked—they're vulgar. Sometimes I've thought perhaps I might do something wicked—I might suddenly fly into a rage and kill Miss Minchin, you know, when she was ill-treating me—but I couldn't be vulgar. Why can't you tell your father I read them?"

"He wants me to read them," said Ermengarde.

"He wants you to know what is in them," said Sara. "And if I can tell it to you in an easy way and make you remember it, I should think he would like that."

"He'll like it if I learn anything in *any* way," said rueful Ermengarde. "You would if you were my father."

"It's not your fault that—" began Sara. She pulled herself up and stopped rather suddenly. She had been going to say, "It's not your fault that you are dull."

"That what?" Ermengarde asked.

"That you can't learn things quickly," amended Sara. "If you can't, you can't. If I can—why, I can. That's all."

As Sara looked at Ermengarde's plump face, one of her wise, old-fashioned thoughts came to her.

"Perhaps," she said, "to be able to learn things quickly isn't everything. To be kind is worth a great deal to other people. If Miss Minchin knew everything on earth and was like what she is now, she'd still be a detestable thing, and everybody would hate her. Lots of clever people have done harm and have been wicked. Look at Robespierre."

She stopped and examined Ermengarde's countenance, which was beginning to look bewildered. "Don't you remember?" she demanded. "I told you about him not long ago. I believe you've forgotten."

"Well, I don't remember all of it," admitted Ermengarde.

"Well, you wait a minute," said Sara, "and I'll take off my wet things and wrap myself in the coverlet and tell you over again."

"Now listen," she said. Sara plunged into the gory records of the French Revolution, and told such stories of it that Ermengarde's eyes grew round with alarm. But though she was rather terrified, there was a delightful thrill in listening, and she was not likely to forget Robespierre again.

It was agreed that Mr. St. John was to be told the plan they had made, and for the present the books were to be left in the attic.

"Now let's tell each other things," said Sara. "How are you getting on with your French lessons?"

"Ever so much better since the last time I came up here and you explained the conjugations. Miss Minchin could not understand why I did my exercises so well."

Sara laughed a little and hugged her knees.

"She doesn't understand why Lottie is doing her sums so well, but it is because she creeps up here, too, and I help her." She glanced round the room. "The attic would be rather nice—if it wasn't so dreadful. It's a good place to pretend in."

The truth was that Ermengarde did not know anything of the sometimes almost unbearable side of life in the attic. Her rare visits there were adventures, and Sara had never confessed to her that at times she was almost ravenous with hunger, as she was tonight. She was growing rapidly, and her constant walking and running about would have given her a keen appetite even if she had had abundant and regular meals. She was growing used to a certain gnawing feeling in her young stomach.

"I suppose soldiers feel like this when they are on a long and weary march," she often said to herself. She liked the sound of the phrase, "long and weary march." She had also a quaint sense of being a hostess in the attic.

"If I lived in a castle," she argued, "and Ermengarde was the lady of another castle and came to see me, with knights and squires and vassals riding with her and banners flying, when I heard the clarions sounding outside the drawbridge I should go down to receive her, and I should spread feasts in the banquet hall and call in minstrels to sing and play and relate romances. When she comes into the attic I can't spread feasts, but I can tell stories." She dispensed generously the one hospitality she could offer—the dreams she dreamed—the visions she saw—the imaginings which were her joy and comfort.

147

So, as they sat together, Ermengarde did not know that she was faint with hunger. Sara felt as if she had never been quite so hungry before.

"I wish I was as thin as you, Sara," Ermengarde said suddenly. "I believe you are thinner than you used to be. Your eyes look so big!"

"I always was a thin child," she said bravely, "and I always had big green eyes."

"I love your queer eyes," said Ermengarde, looking into them with affectionate admiration. "They always look as if they see such a long way. I love them—and I love them to be green—though they look black generally."

"They are cat's eyes," laughed Sara, "but I can't see in the dark with them—because I have tried, and I couldn't."

It was just at this minute that something happened at the sky-light which neither of them saw. If either of them had chanced to turn and look, she would have been startled by the sight of a dark face which peered cautiously into the room and disappeared as quickly and almost as silently as it had appeared. Sara, who had keen ears, suddenly turned a little and looked up at the roof.

"That didn't sound like Melchisedec," she said. "It wasn't scratchy enough."

"What?" said Ermengarde, a little startled.

"It sounded as if something was on the slates—something that dragged softly."

"Could it be—robbers?"

"No," Sara began cheerfully. "There is nothing to steal—"

She broke off in the middle of her words. They both heard Miss Minchin's angry voice. Sara sprang off the bed and put out the candle.

"She is scolding Becky," she whispered, as she stood in the

darkness. "She is making her cry."

"Will she come in here?" Ermengarde whispered back, panic-stricken.

"No. She will think I am in bed. Don't stir."

It was very seldom that Miss Minchin mounted the last flight of stairs. Sara could remember that she had done it only once before. But now she was angry enough to be coming at least part of the way up, and it sounded as if she was driving Becky before her.

"You impudent, dishonest child!" they heard her say. "Cook tells me she has missed things repeatedly."

" 'Twarn't me, mum," said Becky sobbing. "I was 'ungry enough, but 'twarn't me—never!"

"You deserve to be sent to prison," said Miss Minchin's voice. "Picking and stealing! Half a meat pie, indeed!"

" 'Twarn't me," wept Becky. "I could 'ave eat a whole un—but I never laid a finger on it."

Miss Minchin was out of breath, between temper and mounting the stairs. She had intended the meat pie for her special late supper. She boxed Becky's ears.

"Don't tell falsehoods," she said. "Go to your room this instant."

Both Sara and Ermengarde heard the slap, and then heard Becky run in her slipshod shoes up the stairs and into her attic. They heard her door shut, and knew that she threw herself upon her bed.

"I could 'ave e't two of 'em," they heard her cry into her pillow. "An' I never took a bite. 'Twas cook give it to her policeman."

Sara stood in the middle of the room in the darkness. She was clenching her little teeth. She could scarcely stand still, but she dared not move until Miss Minchin had gone down the stairs and all was still.

"The wicked, cruel thing!" she burst forth. "The cook takes things herself and then says Becky steals them. She doesn't! She's so hungry sometimes that she eats crusts out of the ash barrel!" She pressed her hands hard against her face and burst into passionate little sobs, and Ermengarde, hearing this unusual thing, was overawed by it. Sara was crying! The unconquerable Sara! She crept off the bed in the dark and found her way to the table where the candle stood. She struck a match and lit the candle. When she had lighted it, she bent forward and looked at Sara, with her new thought growing to definite fear in her eyes.

"Sara," she said in a timid, almost awe-stricken voice, "are—are—you never told me—I don't want to be rude, but—are *you* ever hungry?"

It was too much just at that moment. The barrier broke down. Sara lifted her face from her hands.

"Yes," she said in a new passionate way. "Yes, I am. I'm so hungry now that I could almost eat *you*. And it makes it worse to hear poor Becky. She's hungrier than I am."

Ermengarde gasped.

"Oh, oh!" she cried woefully. "And I never knew!"

"I didn't want you to know," Sara said. "It would have made me feel like a street beggar. I know I look like a street beggar."

"No, you don't—you don't!" Ermengarde broke in. "Your clothes are a little queer—but you haven't a street-beggar face."

"A little boy once gave me a sixpence for charity," said Sara, with a short little laugh in spite of herself. "Here it is." And she pulled out the thin ribbon hanging from her neck. "He wouldn't have given me his Christmas sixpence if I hadn't looked as if I needed it."

Somehow the sight of the dear little sixpence was good for

both of them. It made them laugh a little, though they both had tears in their eyes.

"Who was he?" asked Ermengarde, looking at it as if it had not been a mere ordinary silver sixpence.

"He was a darling little thing going to a party," said Sara. "He was one of the Large Family, the little one with the round legs, the one I call Guy Clarence. I suppose his nursery was crammed with Christmas presents and hampers full of cakes and things, and he could see I had nothing."

"Oh, Sara!" Ermengarde cried. "What a silly thing I am not to have thought of it!"

"Of what?"

"Something splendid!" said Ermengarde, in an excited hurry. "This very afternoon my nicest aunt sent me a box. It is full of good things. I never touched it, I had so much pudding at dinner, and I was so bothered about Papa's books." Her words began to tumble over each other. "It's got cake in it, and little meat pies, and jam tarts and buns, and oranges and figs and chocolate. I'll creep back to my room and get it this minute, and we'll eat it now."

Sara almost reeled. She clutched Ermengarde's arm.

"Do you think you could?"

"I know I could," answered Ermengarde, and she ran to the door—opened it softly—put her head out into the darkness, and listened. Then she went back to Sara. "The lights are out. Everybody's in bed. I can creep and creep—and no one will hear."

A light sprang into Sara's eyes. "Let us pretend! Let us pretend it's a party! And oh, won't you invite the prisoner in the next cell?"

"Yes! Yes! Let us knock on the wall now. The jailer won't hear."

Sara went to the wall. Through it she could hear poor Becky

crying more softly. She knocked four times.

"That means, 'Come to me through the secret passage under the wall,' " she explained. " ' I have something to communicate.' "

Five quick knocks answered her.

"She is coming," she said.

Almost immediately the door of the attic opened and Becky appeared. Her eyes were red and her cap was sliding off, and when she caught sight of Ermengarde she began to rub her face nervously with her apron.

"Miss Ermengarde has asked you to come in," said Sara, "because she is going to bring a box of good things up here to us."

"To eat, missus?" she said. "Things that's good to eat?"

"Yes," answered Sara, "and we are going to pretend it's a party."

"And you shall have as much as you want to eat," put in Ermengarde. "I'll go this minute!" She was in such haste that as she tiptoed out of the attic she dropped her red shawl.

"Oh, miss! Oh, miss!" Becky gasped. "I know it was you that asked her to let me come. It—it makes me cry to think of it."

In Sara's hungry eyes the old light had begun to glow and transform her world for her. Here in the attic—with the cold night outside—with the afternoon in the sloppy streets barely passed—with the memory of the awful unfed look in the beggar child's eyes not yet faded—this simple, cheerful thing had happened.

She caught her breath.

"Somehow, something always happens," she cried. "Just before things get to the very worst. If I could only just remember that always. The worst thing never quite comes."

She gave Becky a little cheerful shake.

"No, no! You mustn't cry!" she said. "We must make haste and set the table."

152

"Set the table, miss?" said Becky, gazing round the room. "What'll we set it with!"

That moment Sara saw something and pounced upon it. It was Ermengarde's red shawl which lay upon the floor.

"Here's the shawl. It will make such a nice red tablecloth."

They pulled the old table forward, and threw the shawl over it. Red is a wonderfully kind and comfortable color.

"How nice a red rug would look on the floor!" exclaimed Sara. "We must pretend there is one!"

Her eyes swept the bare boards with a swift glance of admiration. The rug was laid down already.

"How soft and thick it is!" she said with a little laugh, and she raised and set her foot down again delicately, as if she felt something under it.

"Yes, miss," answered Becky, watching her with serious rapture.

"What next, now?" said Sara, and she stood still and put her hands over her eyes. "Something will come if I think and wait a little"—in a soft, expectant voice.

One of her favorite fancies was that thoughts were waiting to come to people.

"There!" she cried. "It has come! I know now! I must look among the things in the old trunk I had when I was a princess."

She flew to its corner and knelt down. It had been put in the attic because there was no room for it elsewhere. Nothing had been left in it but rubbish. But she knew she would find something.

In a corner lay a package so insignificant-looking that it had been overlooked. It contained a dozen small white handkerchiefs. She seized them joyfully and ran to the table. She began to arrange them upon the red table-cover, patting and

153

coaxing them into shape with the narrow lace edge curling outward.

"These are the plates," she said. "They are golden plates. These are the richly embroidered napkins. Nuns worked them in convents in Spain."

"Did they, miss?" breathed Becky, her very soul uplifted by the information.

"You must pretend it," said Sara. "If you pretend it enough, you will see them."

Becky shut her eyes and twisted her face in strange convulsive contortions, her hands hanging stiffly clenched at her sides. She looked as if she was trying to lift some enormous weight.

"What is the matter, Becky?" Sara cried. "What are you doing?"

Becky opened her eyes with a start. She answered a little sheepishly, "I was tryin' to see it like you do. I almost did," with a hopeful grin. "But it takes a lot o' stren'th."

"Perhaps it does if you are not used to it," said Sara with friendly sympathy. "But you don't know how easy it is when you've done it often. I wouldn't try so hard just at first. I'll just tell you what things are."

She held an old summer hat in her hand which she had fished out of the bottom of the trunk. There was a wreath of flowers on it. She pulled the wreath off.

"These are garlands for the feast," she said grandly. "They fill all the air with perfume. There's a mug on the wash stand, Becky. Oh, and bring the soap dish for a centerpiece."

Becky handed them to her reverently.

"This is a carven flagon," said Sara, arranging tendrils of the wreath about the mug. "And this—bending tenderly over the soap dish and heaping it with roses—is purest alabaster encrusted with gems."

154

She touched the things gently, a happy smile hovering about her lips, which made her look as if she were a creature in a dream.

"My, ain't it lovely!" whispered Becky.

"If we just had something for bonbon dishes," Sara murmured. "There!"—darting to the trunk again. "I remember I saw something this minute."

It was only a bit of wool wrapped in red and white tissue paper, but the tissue paper was soon formed into little dishes and decoration on the candlestick. Sara drew back and gazed at the old table covered with a red shawl and set with rubbish from a long-unopened trunk, seeing wonders. And Becky, after staring in delight, spoke with bated breath.

"This 'ere," she suggested, with a glance round the attic, "is it the Bastille now, or has it turned into somethin' different?"

"Oh, yes, yes!" said Sara. "Quite different. It is a banquet hall!"

"My eye, miss!" exclaimed Becky. "A blanket 'all!" and she turned to view the splendors about her with awed bewilderment.

"A banquet hall," said Sara. "A vast chamber where feasts are given. It has a vaulted roof, and a minstrels' gallery, and a huge chimney filled with blazing oak logs, and it is brilliant with waxen tapers twinkling on every side."

"My eye, Miss Sara!" gasped Becky again.

Then the door opened, and Ermengarde came in, staggering under the weight of her basket. She entered from the chill darkness outside and found an unexpected party table draped with red, adorned with white, and wreathed with flowers.

"Oh, Sara!" she cried out. "You are the cleverest girl I ever saw."

"But oh, miss," cried Becky, "wait till she's told you what they

155

are! They ain't just—oh, miss, please tell her."

So Sara told her, and made her almost see it all: the golden platters, the vaulted spaces, the blazing logs, the twinkling waxen tapers. As the things were taken out of the basket—the frosted cakes, the fruits, the bonbons—the feast became a splendid thing.

"It's like a real party!" cried Ermengarde.

"It's like a queen's table," sighed Becky.

Then Ermengarde had a sudden brilliant thought.

"I'll tell you what, Sara," she said. "Pretend you are a princess now and this is a royal feast."

"But it's your feast," said Sara. "You must be the princess, and we will be your maids of honor."

"Oh, I can't," said Ermengarde. "I'm too fat, and I don't know how. You be her."

"Well, if you want me to," said Sara.

But suddenly she thought of something else and ran to the rusty grate.

"There is a lot of paper and rubbish stuffed in here!" she exclaimed. "If we light it, there will be a bright blaze for a few minutes, and we shall feel as if it was a real fire." She struck a match and it flared up and illuminated the room.

She stood in the dancing glow and smiled. "Now we will begin the party."

She led the way to the table. She waved her hand graciously to Ermengarde and Becky. She was in the midst of her dream.

"Advance, fair damsels," she said in her happy dream-voice, "and be seated at the banquet table. My noble father, the king, who is absent on a long journey, has commanded me to feast you." She turned her head slightly toward the corner of the room. "What, ho, there, minstrels! Strike up with your viols and bassoons. Princesses," she explained rapidly to

Ermengarde and Becky, "always had minstrels to play at their feasts. Pretend there is a minstrel gallery up there in the corner. Now we will begin."

They had barely had time to take their pieces of cake into their hands—not one of them had time to do more—when they all three sprang to their feet and turned pale faces toward the door, listening.

Someone was coming up the stairs. There was no mistake about it. Each of them recognized the angry, mounting tread and knew that the end of all things had come.

"It's—the missus!" choked Becky, and dropped her piece of cake upon the floor.

"Yes," said Sara, her eyes growing shocked and large in her small white face. "Miss Minchin has found us out."

Miss Minchin struck the door open with a blow of her hand. She was pale herself, but it was with rage. She looked from the frightened faces to the banquet table, and from the banquet table to the last flicker of the burnt paper in the grate.

"I have been suspecting something of this sort," she exclaimed, "but I did not dream of such audacity. Lavinia was telling the truth."

So they knew that Lavinia had somehow guessed their secret and had betrayed them. Miss Minchin strode over to Becky and boxed her ears for a second time.

"You impudent creature!" she said. "You leave the house in the morning!"

Sara stood still, her eyes growing larger, her face paler. Ermengarde burst into tears.

"Oh, don't send her away," she sobbed. "My aunt sent me this food. We're—only—having a party."

"So I see," said Miss Minchin, witheringly. "With the Princess Sara at the head of the table." She turned fiercely on Sara. "It is your doing, I know," she cried. "Ermengarde would never have thought of such a thing. You decorated the table, I suppose—with this rubbish." She stamped her foot at Becky. "Go to your attic!" she commanded, and Becky stole away, her face hidden in her apron, her shoulders shaking.

Then it was Sara's turn again.

"I will attend to you tomorrow. You shall have neither breakfast, dinner, nor supper!"

"I have not had either dinner or supper today, Miss Minchin," said Sara, rather faintly.

"Then all the better. You will have something to remember. Don't stand there. Put those things into the basket again."

Miss Minchin began to sweep them off the table into the basket herself, and caught sight of Ermengarde's new books.

"And you"—to Ermengarde—"have brought your beautiful new books into this dirty attic. Take them up and go back to bed. You will stay there all day tomorrow, and I shall write to your papa. What would he say if he knew where you are tonight?"

Something she saw in Sara's grave, fixed gaze at this moment made her turn on her fiercely.

"What are you thinking of?" she demanded. "Why do you look at me like that?"

"I was wondering," answered Sara, as she had answered that notable day in the schoolroom.

"What were you wondering?"

Sara's manner was only sad and quiet.

"I was wondering," she said in a low voice, "what my papa would say if he knew where I am tonight."

Miss Minchin flew at her and shook her.

"You insolent, unmanageable child!" she cried. "How dare you! How dare you!"

She picked up the books, swept the rest of the feast back into the basket in a jumbled heap, thrust it into Ermengarde's arms, and pushed her before her toward the door.

"I will leave you to wonder," she said. "Go to bed this instant." And she shut the door behind herself and poor stumbling Ermengarde, and left Sara standing alone.

The dream was at an end. The last spark had died out of the paper in the grate. The table was bare. The golden plates and richly embroidered napkins and the garlands were transformed again into old handkerchiefs, scraps of red and white paper, and discarded artificial flowers which lay scattered on the floor. The minstrels in the minstrel gallery had stolen away, and the viols and bassoons were still.

Emily was sitting with her back against the wall, staring very hard. Sara saw her, and went and picked her up with trembling hands.

"There isn't any banquet left, Emily," she said. "And there isn't any princess. There is nothing left but the prisoners in the Bastille." And she sat down and hid her face.

If she had glanced at the skylight she would have been startled by what she would have seen. It was exactly the same face pressed against the glass and peering in at her as had peered in earlier in the evening when she had been talking to Ermengarde.

But she did not look up. She sat with her little black head in her arms for some time. She always sat like that when she was trying to bear something in silence. Then she got up and went slowly to the bed.

"I can't pretend anything else while I am awake," she said. "There wouldn't be any use in trying. If I go to sleep, perhaps a dream will come and pretend for me."

She suddenly felt so tired—perhaps through lack of food—

that she sat down weakly on the edge of the bed.

"Suppose there was a bright fire in the grate, with lots of little dancing flames," she murmured. "Suppose there was a comfortable chair before it—and suppose there was a small table near, with a little hot—hot supper on it. And suppose"—she drew the thin coverings over her—"suppose this was a beautiful soft bed with fleecy blankets and large downy pillows. Suppose—suppose—" And her very weariness was good to her, for her eyes closed and she fell fast asleep.

She did not know how long she slept. But she had been tired enough to sleep deeply and profoundly—too deeply and soundly to be disturbed by anything, even by the squeaks and scamperings of Melchisedec's entire family, if all his sons and daughters had chosen to come out of their hole to fight and tumble and play.

When she awakened it was rather suddenly, and she did not know that any particular thing had called her out of her sleep. The truth was, however, that it was a sound which had called her back—a real sound—the click of the skylight closing after a lithe white figure slipped through it and crouched down just near enough to see what happened in the attic, but not near enough to be seen.

At first she did not open her eyes.

"What a nice dream!" she murmured. "I feel quite warm. I—don't—want—to—wake—up."

Of course it was a dream. She felt as if warm, delightful bedclothes were heaped upon her. She could actually feel blankets, and when she put out her hand it touched something exactly like a satin-covered down quilt. She must not awaken from this delight—she must be quite still and make it last.

But she could not—even though she kept her eyes closed tightly, she could not. Something was forcing her to awaken—

something in the room. It was a sense of light, and a sound—the sound of a crackling, roaring little fire.

"Oh, I am awakening," she said mournfully. "I can't help it—I can't."

Her eyes opened in spite of herself. And then she actually smiled—for what she saw she had never seen in the attic before, and knew she never should see.

"Oh, I haven't awakened," she whispered, daring to rise on her elbow and look all about her. She knew it must be a dream, for if she were awake such things could not be.

This is what she saw. In the grate there was a glowing, blazing fire; on the hob was a little brass kettle hissing and boiling; spread upon the floor was a thick, warm crimson rug; before the fire a folding-chair, unfolded, and with cushions on it; by the chair a small folding-table, unfolded, covered with a white cloth, and upon it spread small covered dishes, a cup, a saucer, a teapot; on the bed were new warm coverings and a satin-covered down quilt; at the foot of the bed a silk robe, a pair of quilted slippers, and some books. The room of her dream seemed changed into fairyland, and it was flooded with warm light, for a bright lamp stood on the table covered with a rosy shade.

She sat up, resting on her elbow, and her breathing came short and fast.

"It does not melt away," she panted. "Oh, I never had such a dream before." She scarcely dared to stir, but at last she pushed the bedclothes aside and put her feet on the floor with a rapturous smile.

"I am dreaming—I am getting out of bed," she heard her own voice say. And then, as she stood up in the midst of it all, turning slowly from side to side—"I am dreaming it stays real! I'm dreaming it feels real. I only think I see it all. It *can't* be true! But oh, how true it seems!"

The blazing fire drew her to it, and she knelt down and held out her hands close to it—so close that the heat made her start back.

"A fire I only dreamed wouldn't be hot," she cried.

She sprang up, touched the table, the dishes, the rug. She went to the bed and touched the blankets. She took up the soft dressing-gown and suddenly clutched it and held it to her cheek.

"It's warm. It's soft!" she almost sobbed. "It's real. It must be!"

She threw it over her shoulders, and put her feet into the slippers.

"They are real, too. It's all real!" she cried. "I am not—I am not dreaming!"

She almost staggered to the books and opened the one which lay on top. Something was written on the flyleaf: "To the little girl in the attic. From a friend."

When she saw that—wasn't it a strange thing for her to do— she put her face down upon the page and burst into tears.

"I don't know who it is," she said, "but somebody cares for me a little. I have a friend."

She took her candle and stole out of her own room and into Becky's, and stood by her bedside.

"Becky, Becky!" she whispered as loudly as she dared. "Wake up!"

Becky wakened and sat upright, her face still smudged with traces of tears. Beside her stood a little figure in a luxurious robe of crimson silk. The face she saw was a shining, wonderful thing. The Princess Sara—as she remembered her—stood at her very bedside, holding a candle in her hand.

"Come," she said. "Oh, Becky, come!"

Becky was too frightened to speak. She simply got up and followed her, with her mouth and eyes open, and without a word.

And when they crossed the threshold, Sara shut the door gently and drew her into the warm, glowing midst of things.

"It's true! It's true!" she cried. "I've touched them all. They are as real as we are. Providence has come and done it, Becky, while we were asleep—Providence that won't let those worst things *ever* quite happen."

16
THE VISITOR

IMAGINE, IF YOU can, what the rest of the evening was like. How they crouched by the fire which blazed and leaped and made so much of itself in the little grate. How they removed the covers of the dishes, and found rich, hot, savory soup which was a meal in itself, and sandwiches and toast and muffins enough for both of them.

"I don't know anyone in the world who could have done it," Sara said, "but there has been someone. And here we are sitting by their fire! And whoever it is—wherever they are—I have a friend, Becky—someone is my friend."

"Do you think," Becky faltered once, in a whisper, "do you think it could melt away, miss? Hadn't we better be quick?" And she hastily crammed her sandwich into her mouth. If it was only a dream, bad manners would be overlooked.

"No, it won't melt away," said Sara. "I am eating this muffin, and I can taste it. You never really eat things in dreams. You only think you are going to eat them. Besides, I keep giving myself pinches. And I touched a hot piece of coal just now, on purpose."

The sleepy comfort which at length almost overpowered them was a heavenly thing. It was the drowsiness of happy, well-fed childhood, and they sat in the fire glow and luxuriated in it until Sara found herself turning to look at her bed.

There were even blankets enough to share with Becky. As she went out of the room, Becky turned upon the threshold and looked about her with devouring eyes.

"If it ain't here in the mornin', miss," she said, "it's been here tonight, anyways, an' I sha'n't never forget it." She looked at each thing, as if to commit it to memory. "The fire was there," pointing with her finger, "an' the table was before it. An' the lamp was there, an' the light looked rosy red. An' there was a satin cover on your bed, an' a warm rug on the floor, an' every-thin' looked beautiful. An' "—she paused a second and laid her hand on her stomach tenderly—"there was soup an' sand-wiches an' muffins—there *was*." And with this reality, she went away.

Through the mysterious news network in schools, it was well known in the morning that Sara Crewe was in horrible dis-grace, that Ermengarde was under punishment, and that Becky was almost packed out of the house before breakfast. The servants knew that she was allowed to stay because Miss Minchin could not easily find another creature helpless and humble enough to work like a slave for so few shillings a week. The older girls in the schoolroom knew why Miss Minchin did not send Sara away.

"She's growing so fast and learning such a lot somehow," said Jessie to Lavinia, "that she will teach classes soon, and Miss Minchin knows she will have to teach for nothing. It was rather nasty of you, Lavvy, to tell about her fun in the attic. How did you find it out?"

"I got it out of Lottie. She's such a baby she didn't know she was telling me. There was nothing nasty about my speaking to Miss Minchin. I felt it my duty. She was being deceitful. And it's ridiculous that she should look so grand and be made so much of in her rags and tatters!"

"What were they doing when Miss Minchin caught them?"

"Pretending some silly thing. Ermengarde had taken up her basket of food to share with Sara and Becky. She never invites us to share things. Not that I care, but it's rather vulgar of her to share with servant girls in attics. I'm surprised Miss Minchin didn't turn Sara out in the cold—even if she does want her for a teacher."

"If she was turned out, where would she go?" inquired Jessie, a trifle anxiously.

"How do I know?" snapped Lavinia. "She'll look rather queer when she comes into the schoolroom this morning, I should think. She had no dinner yesterday, and she's not to have any today."

Jessie was not as ill-natured as she was silly. She picked up her book with a little jerk.

"Well, I think it's horrid," she said. "They've no right to starve her to death."

When Sara went into the kitchen that morning the cook looked askance at her, and so did the housemaids. But she passed them hurriedly. She had overslept a little, and as Becky had done the same, neither had had time to see the other and each had come downstairs in haste.

Sara went into the scullery. Becky was violently scrubbing a kettle and was actually gurgling a little song in her throat. She looked up with a wildly elated face.

"It was there when I wakened, miss—the blanket," she whispered excitedly. "It was as real as it was last night."

"So was mine," said Sara. "It is all there now—all of it. While I was dressing, I ate some of the cold things we left."

"Oh, laws! Oh, laws!" Becky uttered the exclamation in a sort

166

of rapturous groan, and ducked her head over her kettle just in time as the cook came in from the kitchen.

Miss Minchin had expected to see Sara come downstairs with pale cheeks and red eyes and an unhappy, humbled face. Sara had always been an annoying puzzle to her, because severity never made her cry or look frightened. When she was scolded she stood still and listened politely with a grave face. When she was punished she performed her extra tasks or went without her meals with no complaint or outward sign of rebellion. That she never made an impudent answer seemed to Miss Minchin a kind of impudence in itself. But after yesterday's deprivation of meals, the violent scene of last night, the prospect of hunger today, Sara must surely have broken down.

Miss Minchin saw her for the first time when she entered the schoolroom to hear the little French class recite its lessons. She came in with a springing step, color in her cheeks, and a smile hovering about the corners of her mouth. It gave her quite a shock. What was the child made of? She called her at once to her desk.

"You do not look as if you realize that you are in disgrace," she said.

The truth is that when one is still a child—or even if one is grown up—and has been well fed and slept long and softly and warmly, when one has gone to sleep in the midst of a fairy story and has wakened to find it real, one cannot be unhappy or even look as if one were. And one could not, if one tried, keep a glow of joy out of one's eyes.

"I beg your pardon, Miss Minchin," Sara said. "I know that I am in disgrace."

"Be good enough not to forget it and look as if you had come into a fortune. It is an impertinence. And remember you are to have no food today."

"Yes, Miss Minchin," Sara answered. But as she turned away her heart leaped with the memory of what yesterday had been. *If Providence had not saved me just in time*, she thought, *how horrible it would have been!*

"She can't be very hungry," whispered Lavinia spitefully. "Just look at her. Perhaps she is pretending she has had a good breakfast."

"She's different from other people," said Jessie, watching Sara. "Sometimes I'm a bit frightened of her."

"Ridiculous thing!" exclaimed Lavinia.

All through the day the light was in Sara's face and the color in her cheek. The servants cast puzzled glances at her and whispered to each other, and Miss Amelia's small blue eyes wore an expression of bewilderment.

Sara had resolved that the wonders which had happened must be kept secret, if such a thing were possible. It did not seem likely that Miss Minchin should choose to mount to the attic again for some time unless she was led by suspicion. Ermengarde could be told the story and trusted to keep it secret. If Lottie made any discoveries, she could be bound to secrecy also.

"But whatever happens," Sara kept saying to herself all day— "what*ever* happens, somewhere in the world there is a heavenly kind person who is my friend. If I never know who it is—if I never can even thank him—I shall never feel quite so lonely. Oh, Providence was good to me!"

If it was possible for weather to be worse than it had been the day before, it was worse this day—wetter, muddier, colder. There were more errands to be done, the cook was more irritable, and—knowing that Sara was in disgrace—she was more savage. But what does anything matter when Providence has just proved itself one's friend. Sara's supper of the night before had given her strength, and she knew that she would sleep well and warmly. Even though she had naturally begun to be hungry again before evening, she felt that she could bear it until breakfast the following day when her meals would surely be given to her again. It was quite late when she was at last allowed to go upstairs.

When she reached the top flight of stairs and stood before the attic door, her heart beat fast.

"Of course it might all have been taken away," she whispered, trying to be brave. "It might only have been lent to me for just that one night. But it was lent to me. I had it. It was real."

She pushed the door open and went in. Once inside, she gasped slightly, shut the door, and stood with her back against it looking from side to side.

Her heavenly, kind friend had been there again and had done even more than before. The fire was blazing in lovely leaping flames, more merrily than ever. A number of new things had been brought into the attic, which so altered the look of it that if she had not been past doubting she would have rubbed her eyes. Upon the low table another supper stood—this time with cups and plates for Becky as well as herself. A piece of bright, heavy embroidery covered the battered mantel, and on it some ornaments had been placed. All the bare, ugly things which could be covered with draperies had been concealed and made to look quite pretty. Some odd materials of rich colors had been fastened against the wall with tacks so sharp that they could be pressed into the wood and plaster without hammering. Some brilliant fans were pinned up, and there were several large cushions, big enough to use as seats. A wooden box was covered with a rug and some cushions, so that it was like a sofa.

Sara slowly moved away from the door and simply sat down

and looked and looked again.

"It is exactly like something fairy come true," she said. "There isn't the least difference. I feel as if I might wish for anything—diamonds or bags of gold—and they would appear! That wouldn't be any stranger than this. The one thing I always wanted was to see a fairy story come true. I am living in a fairy story. I feel as if I might be a fairy myself, and able to turn things into anything else."

She rose and knocked upon the wall for the prisoner in the next cell, and the prisoner came.

When she entered she almost dropped in a heap upon the floor. For a few seconds she quite lost her breath.

"Oh, laws!" she gasped. "Oh, laws, miss!"

On this night Becky sat on a cushion upon the hearth rug and had a cup and saucer of her own.

When Sara went to bed she found that she had a new thick mattress and big downy pillows. Her old mattress and pillow had been removed to Becky's bedstead, and Becky had been supplied with unheard of comfort.

"Where does it all come from?" Becky broke forth once. "Laws, who does it, miss?"

"Don't let's ask," said Sara. "If it were not that I want to say, 'Oh, thank you,' I would rather not know. It makes it more beautiful."

From that time life became more wonderful day by day. The fairy story continued. Some new comfort or ornament appeared each time Sara opened the door at night, until in a short time the attic was a beautiful little room full of all sorts of odd and luxurious things. The ugly walls were gradually entirely covered with pictures and draperies, clever pieces of folding furniture appeared, a bookshelf was hung up and filled with books, new comforts and conveniences appeared one by one,

From that time life became more wonderful day by day.

until there seemed nothing left to be desired. When Sara went downstairs in the morning, the remains of the supper were on the table. And when she returned to the attic in the evening, her friend had removed them and left another nice little meal. Sara was sent on errands in all weathers and scolded and driven hither and thither. She was scarcely allowed to speak to Ermengarde and Lottie. Lavinia sneered at the increasing shabbiness of her clothes, and the other girls stared curiously at her when she appeared in the schoolroom. But what did it all matter while she was living in this wonderful mysterious story! It was more romantic and delightful than anything she had ever invented. Sometimes, when she was scolded, she could scarcely keep from smiling.

If you only knew! she was saying to herself. *If you only knew!*

The comfort and happiness she enjoyed were making her stronger. If she came home from her errands wet and tired and hungry, she knew she would soon be warm and well fed after she had climbed the stairs. During the hardest day she could occupy herself blissfully by thinking of what she should see when she opened the attic door. In a very short time she began to look less thin. Color came into her cheeks, and her eyes did not seem so much too big for her face.

"Sara Crewe looks wonderfully well," Miss Minchin remarked disapprovingly to her sister.

"Yes," answered poor, silly Miss Amelia. "She was beginning to look like a little starved crow."

"Starved?" exclaimed Miss Minchin angrily. "There was no reason why she should look starved. She always had plenty to eat!"

"Of—of course," agreed Miss Amelia humbly, alarmed to find that she had, as usual, said the wrong thing.

"There is something very disagreeable in seeing that sort of thing in a child of her age," said Miss Minchin vaguely.

"What sort of thing?" Miss Amelia ventured.

"It might almost be called defiance," answered Miss Minchin, feeling annoyed because she knew the thing she resented was nothing like defiance, and she did not know what other unpleasant term to use. "The spirit and will of any other child would have been entirely humbled and broken by—by the changes she has had to submit to. But, upon my word, she seems as if she were a princess."

Even Becky was beginning to look plumper and less frightened. She could not help it. She had her share in the secret fairy story. She had two mattresses, two pillows, plenty of bedcovering, and every night a hot supper and a seat on the cushions by the fire. The Bastille had melted away; the prisoners no longer existed. Two comforted children sat in the midst of delights. Sometimes Sara read aloud from her books, sometimes she learned her own lessons, sometimes she sat and looked into the fire and tried to imagine who her friend could be and wished she could say to him some of the things in her heart.

Then it came about that another wonderful thing happened. A man came to the door and left several parcels. All were addressed in large letters, "To the little girl in the right-hand attic."

Sara herself was sent to open the door and take them in. She laid the two largest parcels on the hall table and was looking at the address, when Miss Minchin came down the stairs and saw her.

"Take the things to the young lady to whom they belong," she said severely. "Don't stand there staring at them."

"They belong to me," answered Sara quietly.

"To you!" exclaimed Miss Minchin. "What do you mean?"

"I don't know where they came from," said Sara, "but they are addressed to me. I sleep in the right-hand attic. Becky has the other one."

Miss Minchin came to her side and looked at the parcels.

"What is in them?" she demanded.

"I don't know," replied Sara.

"Open them," she ordered.

When Sara did as she was told, Miss Minchin's countenance wore an odd expression. She saw pretty and comfortable clothing: shoes, stockings, and gloves, and a warm and beautiful coat. There were even a nice hat and an umbrella. They were all good and expensive things, and on the pocket of the coat was pinned a note, on which were written these words: "To be worn every day. Will be replaced by others when necessary."

Miss Minchin was quite agitated. Could it be that she had made a mistake, after all, and that the neglected child had some powerful though eccentric friend in the background—perhaps some previously unknown relation who had suddenly traced her whereabouts and chose to provide for her in this mysterious and fantastic way? Relations were sometimes very odd—particularly rich old bachelor uncles who did not care for having children near them. A man of that sort might prefer to tend to his young relation's welfare at a distance. Such a person, however, would be sure to be crotchety and hot-tempered enough to be easily offended. It would not be very pleasant if there were such a one, and he should learn all the truth about the thin, shabby clothes, the scant food, and the hard work. She felt very queer and uncertain, and she gave a side glance at Sara.

"Well," she said, in a voice such as she had never used since the little girl lost her father, "someone is very kind to you. As the things have been sent and you are to have new ones when they are worn out, you may as well go and put them on and look respectable. After you are dressed you may come downstairs and learn your lessons in the schoolroom. You need not go out on any more errands today."

About half an hour afterward, when the schoolroom door opened and Sara walked in, the entire school was struck dumb.

"My word!" exclaimed Jessie, jogging Lavinia's elbow. "Look at the Princess Sara!"

It was the Princess Sara indeed. She did not seem the Sara they had seen come down the back stairs a few hours ago. She was dressed in the kind of frock that made Lavinia envious. It was deep and warm in color, and beautifully made. Her hair, whose heavy locks had made her look rather like a Shetland pony when they fell loose about her small face, was tied back with a ribbon.

"Perhaps someone has left her a fortune," Jessie whispered. "I always thought something would happen to her. She is so strange."

"Perhaps the diamond mines have suddenly appeared again," said Lavinia, scathingly.

"Sara," broke in Miss Minchin's deep voice, "come and sit here." And while the whole schoolroom stared with excited curiosity, Sara went to her old seat of honor and bent her head over her books.

That night in her room, after she and Becky had eaten their supper, she sat and looked at the fire seriously for a long time.

"Are you making something up in your head, miss?" Becky inquired with respectful softness. When Sara sat in silence and looked into the coals with dreaming eyes it generally meant that she was making a new story.

"No," she answered. "I am wondering what I ought to do."

Becky stared respectfully. She was filled with something

approaching reverence for everything Sara did and said.

"I can't help thinking about my friend," Sara explained. "I do so want him to know how thankful I am and how happy he has made me. Anyone who is kind wants to know when people have been made happy. They care for that more than for being thanked. I wish—I do wish—"

She stopped short because her eyes at that instant fell upon something standing on a table in a corner. It was a little writing-case fitted with paper and envelopes and pens and ink.

"Oh," she exclaimed, "why did I not think of that before? I can write to him and leave it on the table. Then perhaps the person who takes the things away will take it, too. He won't mind my thanking him, I'm sure."

So she wrote this note:

> I hope you will not think it is impolite that I should write this note to you when you wish to keep yourself a secret. Please believe I do not mean to be impolite or try to find out anything at all; only I want to thank you for being so kind to me—so heavenly kind—and making everything like a fairy story. I am so grateful to you, and I am so happy—and so is Becky. Becky feels just as thankful as I do—it is all just as beautiful and wonderful to her as it is to me. We used to be so lonely and cold and hungry, and now—oh, just think what you have done for us! Please let me say just these words. It seems as if I ought to say them. *Thank* you—*thank* you—*thank* you!
>
> The Little Girl in the Attic

The next morning she left this on the little table, and in the evening it had been taken away with the other things. So she knew her friend had received it. She was reading one of her new books to Becky just before they went to their beds, when her attention was attracted by a sound at the skylight.

"Something's there, miss," Becky whispered.

"Yes," said Sara, slowly. "It sounds like a cat trying to get in."

She left her chair and went to the skylight. It was a strange little sound she heard, like a soft scratching. She suddenly remembered something and laughed. She remembered a quaint little intruder who had made his way into the attic once before. She had seen him that very afternoon, sitting sadly on a table before a window in the Indian gentleman's house.

"Suppose," she whispered, "just suppose it was the monkey who got away again. Oh, I wish it was!"

She climbed on a chair, cautiously raised the skylight, and peeped out. It had been snowing all day, and on the snow, quite near her, crouched a tiny, shivering figure, whose small black face wrinkled itself piteously at sight of her.

"It is the monkey!" she cried out. "He has crept out of the lascar's attic, and he saw the light."

Becky ran to her side.

"Are you going to let him in, miss?" she said.

"Yes," Sara answered joyfully. "It's too cold for monkeys to be out. They're delicate. I'll coax him in."

She put a hand out delicately, speaking in a coaxing voice— as she spoke to the sparrows and to Melchisedec—as if she were some friendly little animal herself.

"Come along, monkey darling," she said. "I won't hurt you."

He knew she would not hurt him. He knew it before she laid her soft, caressing little hand on him and drew him toward her. He had felt human love in the slim brown hands of Ram

177

Dass, and he felt it in hers. He let her lift him through the sky-light, and when he found himself in her arms he cuddled up and looked into her face.

"Nice monkey. Nice monkey," she crooned, kissing his funny head. "Oh, I do love little animal things."

He was evidently glad to get to the fire, and when she sat down and held him on her knee he looked from her to Becky with mingled interest and appreciation.

"He is plain-looking, miss, ain't he?" said Becky.

"He looks like a very ugly baby," laughed Sara. "I beg your pardon, monkey, but I'm glad you are not a baby. Your mother couldn't be proud of you, and no one would dare to say you looked like any of your relations. Oh, I do like you!"

The monkey only put up a tiny paw and scratched his head.

"What shall you do with him?" Becky asked.

"I shall let him sleep with me tonight, and then take him back to the Indian gentleman tomorrow. I am sorry to take you back, monkey, but you must go."

When she went to bed she made him a nest at her feet and he curled up and slept there as if he were a baby.

17
"IT IS THE CHILD"

THE NEXT AFTERNOON three members of the Large Family sat in the Indian gentleman's library doing their best to cheer him up. Today he was waiting anxiously for the return of Mr. Carmichael, whose stay in Moscow had been prolonged from week to week. When he felt at last sure that he had found the right family and had gone to their house, they were absent on a journey. So he had decided to remain in Moscow until their return.

Mr. Carrisford sat in his reclining chair, and Janet sat on the floor beside him. Nora had found a footstool, and Donald was astride the tiger's head on the rug made of the animal's skin. He was riding it rather violently.

"Don't chirrup so loud, Donald," Janet said. "When you come to cheer an ill person up you don't cheer him up at the top of your voice."

"I'm going to be quiet," Donald shouted. "We'll all be as quiet as mice."

"Mice don't make a noise like that," said Janet.

Donald made a bridle of his handkerchief and bounced up and down on the tiger's head.

"A whole lot of mice might," he said cheerfully. "A thousand mice might."

"I don't believe fifty thousand mice would," said Janet, severely, "and we have to be as quiet as one mouse."

Mr. Carrisford laughed and patted her shoulder.

"Papa won't be very long now," she said. "May we talk about the lost little girl?"

"I don't think I could talk much about anything else just now," the Indian gentleman answered, knitting his forehead with a tired look.

"We like her so much," said Nora. "We call her the little *un-fairy* princess."

"Why?" the Indian gentleman inquired.

It was Janet who answered.

"It is because she will be so rich when she is found that she will be like a princess in a fairy tale. We called her the fairy princess at first, but it didn't quite suit."

"Is it true," said Nora, "that her papa gave all his money to a friend to put in a mine that had diamonds in it, and then the friend thought he had lost it all and ran away?"

"But he wasn't a robber, you know," put in Janet, hastily.

The Indian gentleman took hold of her hand quickly. "No, he wasn't really," he said.

"I am sorry for the friend," Janet said. "He didn't mean to do it, and I am sure it would break his heart."

"You are an understanding little woman, Janet," the Indian gentleman said, and he held her hand close.

"Did you tell Mr. Carrisford," Donald shouted again, "about the little-girl-who-isn't-a-beggar? Did you tell him she has new nice clothes? P'r'aps she was lost."

"There's a cab!" exclaimed Janet. "It's stopping before the door. It is Papa!"

They all ran to the windows to look out.

"Yes, it's Papa," Donald proclaimed. "But there is no little girl."

All three of them fled from the room and tumbled into the hall. Mr. Carrisford heard them jumping up and down, clapping their hands, and being caught up and kissed. He made an effort to rise and sank back again.

"It is no use," he said. "What a wreck I am!"

Mr. Carmichael's voice approached the door.

"No, children," he was saying. "You may come in after I have talked to Mr. Carrisford. Go and play with Ram Dass."

Then the door opened and he came in. He looked rosier than ever, and brought an atmosphere of freshness and health with him. But his eyes were disappointed and anxious.

"What news?" Mr. Carrisford asked. "The child the Russian people adopted?"

"She is not the child we are looking for," was Mr. Carmichael's answer. "She is much younger than Captain Crewe's little girl. Her name is Emily Carew. I have seen and talked to her. The Russians were able to give me every detail."

How wearied and miserable the Indian gentleman looked! His hand dropped from Mr. Carmichael's.

"Then the search has to be begun over again," he said. "That is all. Please sit down."

Mr. Carmichael took a seat. He was so well and happy and so surrounded by cheerfulness and love, that desolation and broken health seemed pitiful. If there had been the sound of just one gay little high-pitched voice in the house, it would have been so much less forlorn.

"Come, come," he said in his cheery voice. "We'll find her yet."

"We must begin at once. No time must be lost," Mr. Carrisford fretted. "Have you any new suggestion to make— any whatsoever?"

Mr. Carmichael rose and began to pace the room with a thoughtful, uncertain face.

"Well, perhaps," he said. "I don't know what it may be worth. The fact is, an idea occurred to me as I was thinking the thing over in the train on the journey from Dover."

"What was it? If she is alive, she is somewhere."

"Yes, she is *somewhere*. We have searched the schools in Paris. Let us give up Paris and begin in London. That was my idea—to search London."

"There are schools enough in London," said Mr. Carrisford. Then he slightly started. "By the way, there is one next door."

"Then we will begin there. We cannot begin nearer than next door."

"No," said Carrisford. "There is a child there who interests me, but she is not a pupil. And she is a little dark, forlorn creature, as unlike poor Crewe as a child could be."

Perhaps Providence was at work again at that very moment. It really seemed as if it might be so. What was it that brought Ram Dass into the room with a scarcely concealed touch of excitement in his dark, flashing eyes?

"Sahib," he said, "the child herself has come—the child the sahib felt pity for. She brings back the monkey who had again run away to her attic under the roof. I have asked that she remain. It was my thought that it would please the sahib to see and speak with her."

"Who is she?" inquired Mr. Carmichael.

"God knows," Mr. Carrisford answered. "She is the child I spoke of. A little drudge at the school." He waved his hand to Ram Dass. "Yes, I should like to see her. Go and bring her in." Then he turned to Mr. Carmichael. "While you have been away," he explained, "I have been desperate. The days were so dark and long. Ram Dass told me of this child's miseries, and together we invented a plan to help her. I suppose it was a childish thing to do, but it gave me something to plan and think of. Without the help of an agile, soft-footed Oriental like Ram Dass, however, it could not have been done."

Then Sara came into the room with the monkey in her arms. He was clinging to her and chattering, and the excitement of finding herself in the Indian gentleman's room had brought a flush to Sara's cheeks.

"Your monkey ran away again," she said, in her pretty voice. "He came to my window last night, and I took him in because it was so cold. I would have brought him back if it had not been so late. I knew you were ill and might not like to be disturbed."

The Indian gentleman's hollow eyes dwelt on her with curious interest. "That was very thoughtful of you," he said.

Sara looked toward Ram Dass, who stood near the door. "Shall I give him to the lascar?" she asked.

"How do you know he is a lascar?" said the Indian gentleman, smiling a little.

"Oh, I know lascars," Sara said, handing over the reluctant monkey. "I was born in India."

The Indian gentleman sat upright so suddenly and with such a change of expression that she was for a moment quite startled.

"You were born in India, were you? Come here." And he held out his hand.

Sara went to him and laid her hand in his, as he seemed to want it. She stood still, and her green-gray eyes met his wonderingly. Something seemed to be the matter with him.

"You live next door?" he demanded.

"Yes. I live at Miss Minchin's boarding school."

"But you are not one of her pupils?"

A strange little smile hovered about Sara's mouth. She hesitated a moment.

"I don't think I know exactly what I am," she replied.

"Why not?"

"At first I was a pupil, but now—" The queer little sad smile was on Sara's lips again. "I sleep in the attic, next to the scullery maid. I run errands for the cook. I do anything she tells me, and I teach the little ones their lessons."

"Question her, Carmichael," said Mr. Carrisford, sinking back as if he had lost his strength. "Question her; I cannot."

The big, kind father of the Large Family spoke to her in his nice, encouraging voice.

"What do you mean by 'at first,' my child?" he inquired.

"When I was first taken there by my papa."

"Where is your papa?"

"He died," said Sara, very quietly. "He lost all his money and there was none left for me. There was no one to take care of me or to pay Miss Minchin."

"Carmichael!" the Indian gentleman cried out loudly. "Carmichael!"

"We must not frighten her," Mr. Carmichael said to him in a quick, low voice. And he added aloud to Sara, "So you were sent up into the attic, and made into a little drudge. That was about it, wasn't it?"

"There was no one to take care of me," said Sara. "There was no money. I belong to nobody."

"How did your father lose his money?" the Indian gentleman broke in breathlessly.

"He did not lose it himself," Sara answered, wondering still more each moment. "It was his friend who took his money. He trusted his friend too much."

The Indian gentleman's breath came more quickly. "It might

have happened through a mistake."

"The suffering was just as bad for my papa," she said. "It killed him."

"What was your father's name?" the Indian gentleman said. "Tell me."

"His name was Ralph Crewe," Sara answered. "Captain Crewe. He died in India."

The haggard face contracted, and Ram Dass sprang to his master's side.

"Carmichael," the invalid gasped, "it is the child—the child!"

For a moment Sara thought he was going to die. Ram Dass poured out drops from a bottle and held them to his lips. Sara trembled a little and looked up at Mr. Carmichael.

"What child am I?" she faltered.

"He was your father's friend," Mr. Carmichael answered her. "Don't be frightened. We have been looking for you for two years."

Sara put her hand up to her forehead, and her mouth trembled. She spoke as if she were in a dream.

"And I was at Miss Minchin's all the while," she half whispered. "Just on the other side of the wall."

18
"I TRIED NOT TO BE"

"Upon my word," Mr. Carrisford said faintly to Mr. Carmichael. "I feel as if I do not want to lose sight of her."

"I will take care of her," Janet said, "and mama will come in a few minutes." Janet led her away. "We're so glad you are found," she said to Sara. "You don't know how glad we are that you are found."

Donald stood with his hands in his pockets and gazed at Sara with self-reproachful eyes. "If I'd just asked what your name was when I gave you my sixpence, you would have told me it was Sara Crewe, and you would have been found in a minute."

Then Mrs. Carmichael came in. She took Sara in her arms and kissed her. "You look bewildered, poor child," she said.

Sara could think of only one thing.

"Was he," she said, with a glance toward the closed door of the library, "was he the wicked friend? Oh, do tell me."

Mrs. Carmichael was crying as she kissed her again. She felt as if Sara ought to be kissed often because she had not been kissed for so long.

"He was not wicked, my dear," she answered. "He did not really lose your papa's money. He only thought he had lost it. He almost died of brain fever, and long before he began to

186

recover your poor papa was dead."

"And he did not know where to find me," murmured Sara. "And I was so near."

"He believed you were in school in France," Mrs. Carmichael explained. "And he was continually misled by false clues. He has looked for you everywhere. When he saw you pass by, looking so sad and neglected, he did not dream that you were his friend's poor child. But he was sorry for you and wanted to make you happier. And he told Ram Dass to climb into your attic window and try to make you comfortable."

Sara gave a start of joy; her whole look changed.

"Did Ram Dass bring the things?" she cried out. "Did he tell Ram Dass to do it? Did he make the dream that came true?"

"Yes, my dear—yes! He is kind and good, and he was sorry for you, for little lost Sara Crewe's sake."

The library door opened and Mr. Carmichael appeared. "Mr. Carrisford is better already," he said. "He wants you to come to him."

Sara did not wait. When the Indian gentleman looked at her as she entered, he saw that her face was all alight.

She went and stood before his chair. "You sent the things to me," she said, in a joyful little voice, "the beautiful, beautiful things! You sent them!"

"Yes, I did," he answered. He looked at her with the look she remembered in her father's eyes—that look of loving her and wanting to take her in his arms.

"Then it is you who are my friend," she said. "It is you who are my friend!" And she dropped her face on his thin hand and kissed it.

"The man will be well in three weeks," Mr. Carmichael said to his wife. "Look at his face already." In fact, he did look changed. Here was the "Little Missus," and he had new things

*"You sent the things to me, the beautiful, beautiful things!
You sent them!"*

to think of and plan for already.

In the first place, there was Miss Minchin. Sara was not to return to the girls' school at all. The Indian gentleman was determined upon that point. She must remain where she was, and Mr. Carmichael should go and see Miss Minchin himself.

"I am glad I need not go back," said Sara. "She will be very angry. She does not like me."

But Miss Minchin made it unnecessary for Mr. Carmichael to go to her, by actually coming in search of Sara. She had wanted Sara for something and had heard an astonishing thing. One of the housemaids had seen her steal out with something hidden under her cloak, and had seen her go up the steps next door and enter the house.

"What does she mean?" cried Miss Minchin to Miss Amelia.

"I don't know, I'm sure, sister," answered Miss Amelia. "Unless she has made friends with him because he has lived in India."

"It would be just like her to thrust herself upon him and try to gain his sympathies in some such impertinent fashion," said Miss Minchin. "She must have been in the house for two hours. I will not allow such presumption."

Sara was sitting on a footstool close to Mr. Carrisford's knee and listening to some of the many things he felt it necessary to try to explain to her, when Ram Dass announced the visitor's arrival.

Sara rose involuntarily and became rather pale, but Mr. Carrisford saw that she stood quietly and showed no signs of terror.

Miss Minchin entered the room with a sternly dignified manner. She was correctly and well dressed, and rigidly polite.

"I am sorry to disturb Mr. Carrisford," she said. "I am Miss Minchin, the proprietress of the Young Ladies' Seminary next door."

The Indian gentleman looked at her for a moment in silent scrutiny. He was a man who had naturally a hot temper, and he did not wish it to get the better of him.

"So you are Miss Minchin?" he said.

"I am, sir."

"In that case," the Indian gentleman replied, "you have arrived at the right time. My attorney, Mr. Carmichael, was just on the point of going to see you."

Mr. Carmichael bowed slightly, and Miss Minchin looked from him to Mr. Carrisford in amazement.

"Your attorney!" she said. "I do not understand. I have come here as a matter of duty. I have just discovered that you have been intruded upon through the forwardness of a charity pupil. I came to explain that she intruded without my knowledge." She turned upon Sara. "Go home at once," she commanded indignantly. "You shall be severely punished. Go home at once."

"She is not going."

"Not going?" she repeated.

"No," said Mr. Carrisford. "Her home for the future will be with me."

Miss Minchin fell back in amazed indignation.

"With *you*! With *you*, sir! What does this mean?"

"Kindly explain the matter, Carmichael," said the Indian gentleman, "and get it over as quickly as possible." And he made Sara sit down again, and held her hands in his.

Then Mr. Carmichael explained—in the quiet, level-toned, steady manner of a man who knew his subject and all its legal significance, which Miss Minchin understood as a business woman.

"Mr. Carrisford, madam," he said, "was a friend of the late Captain Crewe. He was his partner in certain large

190

investments. The fortune which Captain Crewe supposed he had lost has been recovered, and is now in Mr. Carrisford's hands."

"The fortune!" cried Miss Minchin, and she really lost color. "Sara's fortune!"

"It *will* be Sara's fortune," replied Mr. Carmichael, rather coldly. "It is Sara's fortune now, in fact. Certain events have increased it enormously. "

"The diamond mines!" Miss Minchin gasped. If this was true, nothing so horrible had ever happened to her since she was born.

"The diamond mines," Mr. Carmichael repeated with a sly, unlawyer-like smile. "There are not many princesses, Miss Minchin, who are richer than your little charity pupil, Sara Crewe. Mr. Carrisford has been searching for her for nearly two years. He has found her at last, and he will keep her."

Miss Minchin was not a clever woman, and in her excitement she was silly enough to make one desperate effort to regain what she had lost through her folly. "I have done everything for her. But for me she should have starved in the streets."

Here the Indian gentleman lost his temper.

"As to starving in the streets," he said, "she might have starved more comfortably there than in your attic."

"Captain Crewe left her in my charge," Miss Minchin argued. "She must return to it until she is of age. She can be a pupil again. She must finish her education. The law will say so."

"Come, come, Miss Minchin," Mr. Carmichael interposed, "the law will do nothing of the sort. If Sara herself wishes to return to you, that rests with Sara."

"Then," said Miss Minchin, "I appeal to Sara. I have not spoiled you, perhaps," she said awkwardly to the little girl, "but you know that your papa was pleased with your progress. And—ahem—I have always been fond of you."

Sara's green-gray eyes fixed themselves on her with the quiet, clear look Miss Minchin particularly disliked.

"Have you, Miss Minchin?" she said. "I did not know that."

Miss Minchin reddened and drew herself up.

"You ought to have known it," said she. "But children, unfortunately, never know what is best for them. Amelia and I always said you were the cleverest child in the school. Will you not do your duty to your poor papa and come home with me?"

Sara took a step toward her and stood still. She was thinking of the day when she had been told that she belonged to nobody and was in danger of being turned into the street. She was thinking of the cold, hungry hours she had spent alone with Emily and Melchisedec in the attic. She looked Miss Minchin steadily in the face.

"You know why I will not go home with you, Miss Minchin," she said. "You know quite well."

A hot flush showed itself on Miss Minchin's hard, angry face.

"You will never see your companions again," she began. "I will see that Ermengarde and Lottie are kept away—"

Mr. Carmichael stopped her with polite firmness.

"Excuse me," he said. "She will see anyone she wishes to see. The parents of Miss Crewe's fellow-pupils are not likely to refuse her invitations."

Miss Minchin flinched. Most people would not refuse to allow their children to remain friends with a little heiress of diamond mines. And if Mr. Carrisford chose to reveal to them how unhappy Sara Crewe had been made, many unpleasant things might happen.

"You have not undertaken an easy charge," she said to the Indian gentleman, as she turned to leave the room. "The child is neither truthful nor grateful. I suppose"—to Sara—"that you feel now that you are a princess again."

Sara looked down and flushed a little.

"I—tried not to be anything else," she answered in a low voice—"even when I was coldest and hungriest—I *tried* not to be."

"Now it will not be necessary to try," said Miss Minchin acidly, as Ram Dass ushered her out of the room.

She returned home to her sitting room and sent at once for Miss Amelia. Poor Miss Amelia sat with her there all afternoon, and shed a good many tears and mopped her eyes a good deal. One of her unfortunate remarks almost caused her sister to snap her head entirely off.

"I'm not as clever as you, sister," she said, "and I am always afraid to say things to you for fear of making you angry. I often thought it would have been better if you had been less severe on Sara Crewe, and had seen that she was decently dressed and more comfortable. I *know* she was worked too hard for a child of her age, and I know she was only half fed."

"How dare you say such a thing!" exclaimed Miss Minchin.

"I don't know how I dare," Miss Amelia answered, with a kind of reckless courage, "but now I've begun I may as well finish, whatever happens to me. The child was a clever child and a good child—and she would have paid you for any kindness you had shown her. But you didn't show her any. The fact was, she was too clever for you, and you always disliked her for that reason. She used to see through us both—"

"Amelia!" gasped her infuriated elder, looking as if she would box her ears and knock her cap off, as she had often done to Becky.

But Miss Amelia's disappointment had made her hysterical enough not to care what occurred next.

"She did! She did!" she cried. "She saw through us both. She saw that you were a hard-hearted, worldly woman, and that I was a weak fool, and that we were both of us willing to grovel on our knees for her money, and behave ill to her when it was taken from her—though she behaved herself like a little princess even when she was a beggar. She did—she did—like a little princess!" And her hysterics got the better of the poor woman, and she began to laugh and cry both at once, and rock herself backward and forward.

"And now you've lost her!" she cried wildly. "Some other school will get her and her money, and if she were like any other child she'd tell how she's been treated, and all our pupils would be taken away and we should be ruined. And it serves us right; but it serves you right more than it does me. Maria Minchin, you're a hard, selfish, worldly woman!"

And she was in danger of making so much noise with her hysterical chokes and gurgles that her sister was obliged to calm her.

And from that time forward, the elder Miss Minchin actually began to stand a little in awe of a sister who was evidently not quite so foolish as she looked, and might, consequently, break out and speak truths people did not want to hear.

That evening when the pupils were gathered together before the fire in the schoolroom, as was their custom before going to bed, Ermengarde came in with a letter in her hand and a queer expression on her round face. It was queer because it was an expression of delighted excitement combined with shocked amazement.

"What is the matter?" cried two or three voices at once.

"Is it anything to do with the quarrel that has been going on?" said Lavinia, eagerly. "Miss Amelia has had something like hysterics and has had to go to bed."

Ermengarde answered them slowly as if she were half stunned.

"I have just had this letter from Sara," she said, holding it out to let them see what a long letter it was.

"From Sara!" Every voice joined in that exclamation.

"Where is she?" Jessie almost shrieked.

"Next door," said Ermengarde, "with the Indian gentleman."

"Where? Has she been sent away? Does Miss Minchin know? Was the quarrel about that? Why did she write? Tell us! Tell us!"

There was a perfect babel, and Lottie began to cry. Ermengarde answered them slowly.

"There were diamond mines," she said stoutly. "There were!"

Open mouths and open eyes confronted her.

"They were real," she hurried on. "It was all a mistake about them. Something happened for a time, and Mr. Carrisford thought they were ruined—"

"Who is Mr. Carrisford?" shouted Jessie.

"The Indian gentleman. And Captain Crewe thought so, too—and he died. And Mr. Carrisford had brain fever and ran away, and he almost died. And he did not know where Sara was. And it turned out that there were millions and millions of diamonds in the mines, and half of them belong to Sara. They belonged to her when she was living in the attic with no one but Melchisedec for a friend, and the cook ordering her about. And Mr. Carrisford found her this afternoon, and he has got her in his home—and she will never come back—and she will be more a princess than she ever was—a hundred and fifty thousand times more. And I am going to see her tomorrow afternoon. There!"

Even Miss Minchin could scarcely have controlled the uproar after this, and though she heard the noise, she did not try. She was not in the mood to face anything more than she was facing in her room, while Miss Amelia was weeping in bed. She knew the news had penetrated the walls in some mysterious manner, and that every servant and every child would go to bed talking about it.

So until almost midnight the entire school, realizing somehow that all rules were laid aside, crowded round Ermengarde and read and reread the letter containing a story which was as wonderful as any Sara herself had ever invented, and which had the amazing charm of having happened to Sara herself in the very next house.

Becky, who had heard it also, managed to creep upstairs earlier than usual. She wanted to get away from people and go and look at the little magic room once more. It was not likely that it would be left for Miss Minchin. It would be taken away, and the attic would be bare and empty again. Glad as she was for Sara's sake, she went up the last flight of stairs with a lump in her throat and tears blurring her sight. There would be no fire tonight, and no rosy lamp. No supper, and no princess sitting in the glow reading or telling stories—no princess!

She choked down a sob as she pushed the attic door open, and then she broke into a low cry.

The lamp was flushing the room, the fire was blazing, the supper was waiting, and Ram Dass was standing smiling into her startled face.

"Missee sahib remembered," he said. "She wished you to know the good fortune which has befallen her. Behold a letter on the tray. She has written. She did not wish that you should go to sleep unhappy. The sahib commands you to come to him tomorrow. You are to be the attendant of missee sahib. Tonight I take these things back over the roof."

And having said this with a beaming face, he made a little bow and slipped through the skylight with an agile silentness which showed Becky how easily he had done it before.

19
ANNE

NEVER HAD SUCH joy reigned in the nursery of the Large Family. Never had they dreamed of such delights as resulted from the little-girl-who-was-not-a-beggar. The mere fact of her sufferings and adventures made her a priceless possession. Everybody wanted to be told over and over again the things that had happened to her. When one was sitting by a warm fire in a big, glowing room, it was quite delightful to hear how cold it could be in an attic.

Of course the story loved best was the banquet and the dream that was true. Sara told it for the first time the day after she had been found to several members of the Large Family who came to take tea with her. As they sat on the hearth-rug she told the story and the Indian gentleman listened and watched. When she had finished, she looked up at him and put her hand on his knee.

"That is my part," she said. "Now won't you tell your part of it, Uncle Tom?" He had asked her to call him always Uncle Tom. "I don't know your part yet, and it must be beautiful."

So he told them how Ram Dass had tried to distract him when he was ill and irritable by describing the passers-by, and there was one child who passed more often than any one else.

He had begun to be interested in her, partly because he was thinking a great deal of a little girl and partly because Ram Dass had told about his visit to the attic to chase the monkey. Bit by bit, Ram Dass had made discoveries concerning the wretchedness of the little girl's life.

"Sahib," he had said one day, "I could cross the roof and make the child a fire when she is out on some errand. When she returned, wet and cold, she would think an unknown friend had done it."

Mr. Carrisford's sad face had lighted with a smile, and Ram Dass explained how simple it would be to accomplish numbers of other things. The preparations for carrying out the plan had filled many a day with interest which would otherwise have dragged wearily. On the night of the banquet, Ram Dass had kept watch, all his packages being in readiness in his own attic. His helper had waited with him, as interested as himself in the odd adventure. Ram Dass had been lying flat upon the slates, looking in at the skylight, when Ermengarde's banquet had come to its disastrous conclusion. He had observed Sara's wearied sleep, and then, with a dark lantern, he had crept into the room while his companion remained outside and handed things to him. The children asked a thousand questions.

"I am so glad it was you who were my friend!" Sara said to Uncle Tom.

There never were such friends as these two became. The Indian gentleman had never had a companion he liked as much as he liked Sara. In a month's time he was a new man. He was always amused and interested. There was a little joke between them that he was a magician, and it was one of his pleasures to invent things to surprise her. She found beautiful new flowers growing in her room, little gifts tucked under pillows, and once, as they sat together in the evening, they heard the scratch of a heavy paw on the door. When Sara went to find out what it was, there stood a great dog—a splendid Russian boarhound—with a grand silver and gold collar bearing an inscription. "I am Boris," it read. "I serve the Princess Sara."

There was nothing the Indian gentleman loved more than the recollection of the little princess in rags and tatters. The afternoons in which the Large Family or Ermengarde and Lottie gathered to rejoice together were delightful. But the hours when Sara and the Indian gentleman sat alone and read or talked had a special charm of their own. Many interesting things occurred.

One evening Mr. Carrisford looked up from his book and noticed that his companion sat gazing into the fire.

"What are you supposing, Sara?" he asked.

Sara looked up, with a bright color on her cheek. "I *was* supposing," she said. "I was remembering that hungry day, and a child I saw."

"But there were a great many hungry days," said the Indian gentleman, with a sad tone in his voice. "Which hungry day was it?"

"It was the day the dream came true."

Then she told him the story of the bun shop and the fourpence she picked up out of the sloppy mud, and the child who was hungrier than herself. She told it simply and in as few words as possible, but somehow the Indian gentleman found it necessary to shade his eyes with his hand and look down at the carpet.

"And I was supposing a kind of plan," she said, when she had finished. "I was thinking I should like to do something."

"What was it?" said Mr. Carrisford, in a low tone. "You may do anything you like to do, princess."

"I was wondering—" Sara hesitated. "You know, you say I have so much money—I was wondering if I could go to see the bun-woman and tell her that when hungry children—particularly on those dreadful days—come and sit on the steps or look in at the window, she should just call them in and give them something to eat, and send the bills to me. Could I do that?"

"You shall do it tomorrow morning," said the Indian gentleman.

"Thank you," said Sara. "You see, I know what it is to be hungry, and it is very hard when one cannot even pretend it away."

"Yes, yes, my dear," said the Indian gentleman. "Yes, yes, it must be. Try to forget it. Come and sit on this footstool near my knee, and only remember you are a princess."

"Yes," said Sara, smiling, "and I can give buns and bread to the populace."

The next morning Miss Minchin saw from her window the things she perhaps least enjoyed seeing. The Indian gentleman's carriage with its tall horses drew up before the door of the next house, and its owner and a familiar little figure, warm with soft, rich furs, descended the steps to get into it. It was followed by another as familiar, the sight of which she found very irritating. It was Becky, who always accompanied her young mistress to her carriage, carrying wraps and belongings. Already Becky had a pink, round face.

A little later the carriage drew up before the door of the baker's shop, and its occupants got out just as the bun-woman was putting a tray of smoking-hot buns into the window.

When Sara entered the shop, the woman turned and looked at her, and came and stood behind the counter. For a moment she looked at Sara very hard indeed, and then her good-natured face lighted up.

"I'm sure that I remember you, miss," she said. "And yet—"

"Yes," said Sara; "once you gave me six buns for fourpence, and—"

"And you gave five of 'em to a beggar child," the woman broke in on her. "I've always remembered it." She turned round to the Indian gentleman and spoke her next words to him. "I beg your pardon, sir, but there's not many young people that notices a hungry face in that way. I've thought of it many a time. Excuse the liberty, miss, but you look rosier and—well, better than you did that—that—"

"I am better, thank you," said Sara. "And I am much happier, and I have come to ask you to do something for me."

"Me, miss!" exclaimed the bun-woman, smiling cheerfully. "Why, bless you! Yes, miss. What can I do?"

And then Sara, leaning on the counter, made her little proposal concerning the dreadful days and the hungry waifs and the buns.

The woman watched her and listened with an astonished face.

"Why, bless me!" she said again when she had heard it all, "it'll be a pleasure to me to do it. I am a working-woman myself and cannot afford to do much on my own account, and there's sights of trouble on every side. But if you'll excuse me, I'm bound to say I've given away many a bit of bread since that wet afternoon, just thinking of you—an' how wet an' cold you was an' how hungry you looked. An' yet you gave away your hot buns as if you was a princess."

The Indian gentleman smiled involuntarily at this, and Sara smiled a little, too, remembering what she had said to herself when she put the buns down on the ravenous child's ragged lap.

"She looked so hungry," she said. "She was even hungrier than I was."

"She was starving," said the woman. "Many's the time she's told me of it—how she sat there in the wet and felt as if a wolf was a-tearing at her poor young insides."

"Oh, have you seen her since then?" exclaimed Sara. "Do you know where she is?"

"Yes, I do," answered the woman, smiling more good-naturedly than ever. "Why, she's in that there back room, miss, an' has been for a month. An' a decent, well-meanin' girl she's goin' to turn out, an' such a help to me in the shop an' in the kitchen as you'd scarce believe, knowin' how she's lived."

She stepped to the door of the little back parlor and spoke, and the next minute a girl came out and followed her behind the counter. It was the beggar-child, clean and neatly clothed, and looking as if she had not been hungry for a long time. She looked shy, but she had a nice face now that the wild look had gone from her eyes. She knew Sara in an instant, and stood and looked at her as if she could never look enough.

"You see," said the woman, "I told her to come when she was hungry, and when she'd come I'd give her odd jobs to do. An' I found she was willing, and somehow I got to like her. The end of it was, I've given her a job an' a home, and she helps me, an' behaves well, an' is as thankful as a girl can be. Her name's Anne. She has no other."

The children stood and looked at each other for a few minutes, and then Sara took her hand out of her muff and held it out across the counter. Anne took it, and they looked straight into each other's eyes.

"I am so glad," Sara said. "And I have just thought of something. Perhaps Mrs. Brown will let you be the one to give the buns and bread to the children. Perhaps you would like to do it because you know what it is to be hungry."

"Yes, miss," said the girl.

And somehow Sara felt as if she understood her, though she said so little and only stood still and looked and looked after her as she went out of the shop with the Indian gentleman, and they got into the carriage and drove away.

About the author and *A Little Princess*

Frances Hodgson Burnett (1849–1924) was a born storyteller. Even when she was a young child living in Manchester, England, her greatest pleasure was in making up stories and acting them out, using her dolls as characters. When she was sixteen, she was brought from England to Tennessee by her fatherless, poverty-stricken family. There she started to write stories in a cold little attic room, and they eventually made her famous. She published more than fifty books, but the most beloved are *Little Lord Fauntleroy*, *The Secret Garden*, and *A Little Princess*. She said of herself, "With the best that was in me, I have tried to write more happiness into the world."

"I met little princess Sara Crewe when I was nine years old and we quickly became best friends. We had a lot in common—fathers whose work took them away from us, love of books and beautiful things, financial hardship, and mistreatment by unkind people. Sara understood me. She also taught me about courage, kindness, determination, and hope. She helped me believe that dreams really do come true, that God and his human helpers somehow always find ways to deliver delightful surprises into the dark places of our lives." —Ranelda Mack Hunsicker, author of *Secrets* and *The Hidden Price of Greatness*

About the editor

Kathryn Lindskoog, an educator, literary critic, and expert on C. S. Lewis, has written more than twenty books. Among them are *C. S. Lewis: Mere Christian*; *A Child's Garden of Christian Verses* and *How to Grow a Young Reader.* She earned her B.A. at the University of Redlands and her M.A. at California State University at Long Beach. In addition to teaching high-school English for seven years, she has taught as an adjunct instructor at Seattle Pacific University, Biola University, New Orleans Baptist Seminary, and Fuller Theological Seminary. Her teaching career has been limited by multiple sclerosis, which became disabling in the 1960s. Lindskoog is married with two grown sons. She lives in Orange, California.

About the illustrator

Barbara Chitouras has been a freelance artist for almost twenty years, creating artwork for children's books, textbooks, and rubber stamp designs. She studied at Massachusetts College of Art in Boston and has a B.A. in Illustration. She currently lives in the Boston area.